Paula stood at her post on the chicken line in the Chaco Chicken plant. The carcasses entered this room impaled on stainless steel rods, and the workers were supposed to slice the carcasses open and remove the innards as they spilled out. Paula did this hundreds of times every day, and she was good at it. One of the best workers in the plant.

But Paula wasn't feeling like herself today. She caught herself zoning out as two or three chickens passed by.

Concentrate, she told herself. But the chickens kept zooming by her as she tried, in vain, to do her job. Slice, scoop. Slice, scoop. Slice –

Paula dropped her knife and screamed.

Instead of another chicken carcass jammed onto the next steel rod, a human head sat there – blood dripping from the opening where the neck used to be.

Other X-Files books in this series

Voyager

THE X FILES™

Our Town

Novelization by Eric Elfman

Based on the television series
The X-Files created by
Chris Carter

Based on the teleplay
written by Frank Spotnitz

HarperCollins*Publishers*

Voyager
An Imprint of HarperCollins*Publishers*
77–85 Fulham Palace Road,
Hammersmith, London W6 8JB

This paperback edition 1997
   2 3 4 5 6 7 8 9

First published in the USA by HarperTrophy
A division of HarperCollins*Publishers* 1997

ISBN 0 00 648327 5

Set in Goudy

Printed and bound in Great Britain by
Caledonian International Book Manufacturing Ltd, Glasgow

Chapter One

It's a funny thing, darkness.

Sometimes it can be comforting. Like the darkness under the covers when you were a kid, when you pulled your blanket over your head to hide from the ghosts and vampires you imagined were waiting to pounce.

Sometimes it can be frightening. Like the darkness in the basement of the old house you used to live in, where it was inky black—even in the daytime.

And sometimes it can be lonely. Like the darkness you face near midnight, as you drive the deserted roads on the outskirts of town, wondering where it had all gone wrong.

George Kearns, reviewing his life, absently turned the steering wheel to follow the gentle curve in the road skirting the edge of town.

The darkness outside, beyond the narrow beams of his headlights, perfectly matched his mood.

How had it come to this?

He was a decent man—and for nearly fifty years, he had led a decent life.

Now he was about to lose his job—of that he was certain. George was good at his work. But his competence as a poultry inspector wasn't the issue. Walt Chaco, the owner of the chicken-processing plant, was the issue. Mr. Chaco wanted him gone. George could feel it every time the older man passed, every time they spoke. Mr. Chaco had a way of looking George over—it made him feel like he was being sized up, his *own* quality being inspected. And no doubt found lacking.

Now his bosses back in Washington were making a fuss. You'd think he'd be congratulated, commended, for doing such an excellent job inspecting poultry. He was, after all, protecting the public. But no. They were going to recall him—he could feel it. George knew the way it worked: Deals had already been struck, understandings reached. The plant would continue to operate in an unsanitary manner and George would be "relocated"—again. He was sure they were already whispering about it in town.

In town . . .

Dudley, Arkansas, had never accepted him. Ever since he and his wife had moved to Dudley six months ago, George could sense people of the small town eyeing him, judging him, weighing him. George knew it wasn't his imagination, although he couldn't quite put his finger on what was wrong. His work took him to plenty of towns, some friendly, some not, but he'd never encountered anything like this. The treatment he got in Dudley was downright hostile at times. He was an outsider, and the townspeople weren't about to let him forget that.

It was different for his wife. She had fit right in, practically from day one. It was almost eerie—like Doris had always belonged here.

Doris. George focused his thoughts on his

wife. That was a whole other problem. Their marriage had started coming unglued in the past few months. All of a sudden it was as if she could barely stand to look at him. When he touched her it was like touching stone. But when did it start to go wrong between them? And why?

Driving his car, feeling the darkness, George became aware of the wetness on his cheeks. He didn't know he had been crying. He hadn't realized until that very moment how incredibly unhappy he had become.

"What's the matter, George?"

The voice shocked George back to the present. He had been so wrapped up in his own thoughts, he had nearly forgotten he wasn't alone. George glanced over at the woman in the seat next to him.

At Paula Gray.

She had been sitting there so quietly— probably wrapped up in thoughts of her own. Probably wondering what she was doing in a car, so late at night, with a married man.

George glanced at her again. He didn't

know her age for sure, but he guessed she must be just shy of twenty. Her shimmering auburn hair hung just past her shoulders, and her skin was clear and smooth. She was a beautiful young girl.

"Is something wrong?" Paula persisted.

"No, nothing," George answered. "Just thinking." He pretended to scratch an itch on his cheek as he wiped away the tears.

"What about?" Paula asked, coyly.

"About what I'm doing here," George muttered, too softly for her to hear.

Loneliness will make a man do crazy things, George reckoned. It had begun as an innocent flirtation at work. For some reason Paula had responded to George's advances. Maybe she felt sorry for him or something, but over the course of weeks, they had begun spending more time with each other. First their coffee breaks. Then their lunches.

Now this.

And this was a serious mistake, George realized. This was no way to go about winning back his wife, his job, or his self-respect. He had to end it before it began.

"Stop right here," Paula said, pointing to the side of the road. "Park here."

The cold brilliance of the headlights flooded the glade in front of them. They had reached a narrow strip of woods at the edge of the town.

George pulled over and parked the car, thinking about what he would say, how he would break it to her.

He would tell her that they were both making a terrible mistake. He would tell her how much he loved his wife. If she started to cry, he would tell her that she was a beautiful young girl who could have her pick of any boy in town. That she didn't need an old man like him.

"I—" George began, but his throat was tightening, and he was finding it difficult to get the words out. "I just—"

"Come on," Paula said, smiling at him. "Let's go into the woods."

George opened his mouth again, intending to explain tenderly but forcefully why it could not, should not, would not be . . . but nothing came out. A pressure rising in his chest had paralyzed him—it was a feeling he immediately, and hopelessly, recognized. And George realized that he wasn't going to be telling Paula anything. Not right now.

He was having another attack.

Paula opened her door and slid out of the car before George could utter another word.

"You coming?" she asked, giggling, as she disappeared into the darkness.

Not an attack right now, George prayed—but it was too late. He knew with certainty what was coming next. And sure enough, a cold and furious fire suddenly swept from his scalp to his soles, and his body was wracked by painful, violent shudders.

Gritting his teeth, George managed, by sheer force of will, to reach inside his jacket pocket and take out a small vial.

The shocks were subsiding, but that didn't mean the attack was over, George knew. They could go away at this point, or come back for a second, and even a third, wave. He quickly twisted the cap off the vial, and shook two white tablets into his trembling palm.

George lifted his hand to his open mouth and tossed in the pills. Water would be good, he thought, grimacing as he ground the pills to a bitter powder between his teeth. Dr. Randolph at the plant had prescribed them—he'd said the painful tremors were just caused by stress. Well, maybe so—he was sure under a lot of stress right now.

George could sense the attack ending. It had lasted only a few seconds, but those painful seconds felt more like an eternity. Taking a deep breath, he opened his door and tumbled out of the car. He looked in the direction that Paula had disappeared, but all he could see was a thick tangle of trees.

"Paula!" he called. "Paula! Where are you?"

"Over here, George! Come on!"

George could hear her voice coming from deep within the woods. He unhappily realized what he had to do now. Scowling, George started toward the trees.

"All right, Paula!" he called out again. "I'm

coming! Which way?"

"Over here, George! Hurry!"

Her voice floated to him through the forest, and he followed it, starting to trot. Overweight and far from fit, he was soon sweating from the exertion. His heavy puffs of breath condensed in the damp night air, becoming a vapor trail that hung behind him.

"Come on, George . . ." He could hear Paula's tinkling laughter just up ahead.

George struggled up a low hill, through some brambles and low bushes. The darkness inside the woods was nearly complete. As he moved toward her voice, he kept his hands out in front of him, swatting at branches as he stumbled along.

"Paula," he cried plaintively, as he entered a small clearing. "Where are you? I'm too old for these kinds of—*oof!*" He had meant to say "games" as he tripped over a thick root and nose-dived into the hard ground.

George stayed down for a moment, gasping for breath. Slowly, shakily, he got to his knees. A few inches away he saw a swarm of fireflies. He blinked his eyes and refocused. No, they weren't inches away—they were all the way across the clearing.

And they weren't fireflies.

They were balls of bouncing light. Dozens of them.

Coming his way.

George rose unsteadily to his feet. He didn't know what they were, and didn't want to know. He didn't know where Paula was, either, and at this point he didn't care. All he wanted to do was to get out of these woods.

He turned as he heard a rustling behind him.

"Paula? Paula, is that you?"

Suddenly the branches parted, and an enormous face stared back at him, inches from his own.

But it wasn't a human face—it was some sort of grotesque mask. The head was surrounded by a blur of fiery red. Angry streaks of yellow were splayed across its cheeks. The hideous thing's eyes and mouth were outlined in a white so bright, they shone even in the dark.

George, too frightened to make a sound, took an involuntary step back.

Then he saw the ax.

The monster lifted the weapon high over George's head, and George finally managed to let out a scream. Then they were both screaming as the creature plunged the ax down toward George's throat.

Only George's scream stopped when the ax drove home, as all the lights went out and his world was plunged into yet another kind of darkness . . .

Chapter Two

Scully parked her car beneath the J. Edgar Hoover office building, headquarters of the FBI.

She stepped into the elevator and smiled warmly at the new agent she saw standing there, a young woman she had met just the day before. But the new agent quickly looked away, her gaze fixed firmly on the row of floor numbers over the elevator door.

Scully's smile faded as the doors closed. *Well, that didn't take long,* she thought. She wondered who among her colleagues had the distinction of being the first to break the news that Scully was . . . well, different. Weird. That the cases she investigated weren't normal. Who knew what the young woman had heard? That Scully has been on board a flying saucer? That she vacations at Loch Ness? That she's dating Bigfoot?

The elevator reached the basement almost immediately. As Scully stepped out onto her floor, she could hear the woman's sigh of relief behind her, not quite masked by the sigh of the elevator doors sliding closed.

Scully walked briskly down the dimly lit corridor, quickly reaching the door of Mulder's office. She pushed it open and stepped into the L-shaped room.

Her partner was intently studying the contents of a folder laid open on his desk.

"Glad you could make it," Fox Mulder said, without looking up.

Scully glanced up at the clock. Ten minutes to nine. She was early—just not as early as he was. She dropped her bag under the desk and turned to him with arms folded.

She couldn't blame him for the attitude of her co-workers. It was her choice to stay here. To keep investigating the kinds of cases that Mulder was interested in. Cases nobody else would touch.

"What is it?" Scully finally asked, nodding to the file on Mulder's desk.

Mulder leaned back in his chair and rubbed his eyes. Then he picked up the folder and handed it over the desk to his partner. "Here. Let me know what you think."

Scully opened the folder and, as she scanned the pages, became more and more puzzled.

It was a simple missing-persons case.

There was no UFO connection, not a whiff of the supernatural, no link to the un-explained. There was absolutely nothing here that would interest Fox Mulder. Of all the unsolved mysteries in the FBI's files, why was this one worth his attention?

She looked up at her partner, and tried to read his expression, but it was as noncom-mittal as ever. What did he see in this case that she had missed?

She flipped back to the top page in the file and reread the original missing-persons report, more slowly this time.

The man's name was George Kearns. He had vanished without a trace over ten weeks ago. If there ever had been a trail, it was sure to be cold by now.

Scully shook her head. "Mulder, you want to know what I think? I think it's a wild-goose chase."

Mulder stared straight at his partner. "Chicken," he said.

Scully was surprised that he would call her that—and a little bit hurt. Did he really think she was afraid? Of *this* case? She opened her mouth to protest, but Mulder had read her expression, and hurried to correct her mistaken impression.

"You mean a wild-*chicken* case. George Kearns was a federal poultry inspector assigned to Dudley, Arkansas—home of the famous Chaco Chicken factory."

Scully wasn't amused. "And he up and left over two months ago. Why are *you* interested in *this* case?"

Mulder let the question roll over him, and cocked his head—almost as though he was wondering the same thing himself. "A couple of reasons," he said slowly. "Did you see the supplemental police report? On the night George Kearns disappeared, a woman on I-40 claimed she saw a strange fire in an adjacent field."

"I read that," Scully replied, nodding. "She called it *foxfire*."

"Foxfire spirits—they're part of the folklore of the Ozarks, dating back to the nineteenth century." Mulder leaned forward, and Scully could see the storyteller gleam in his eyes. "Many people claimed—some swore in court, even—that they watched, helplessly, as their kinfolk were dragged off by fireballs. The bodies were never found. They called it foxfire. Some of them believed it was really the avenging spirits of massacred Indians."

So there was a supernatural connection after all, Scully realized. But a pretty weak one.

"Mulder, did you check to see if that woman called Oprah after she filed her police report?" Scully asked sarcastically.

Mulder reached over to the folder in Scully's hand, and flipped through the pages to a photograph of a field. In the image, a state trooper crouched on the ground. He was holding a tape measure over a huge black circle that had been charred into the earth.

"Most legends don't leave twelve-foot burn marks," Mulder said dryly. "This is the field where the woman claimed she saw the foxfire. This picture was taken the next day."

"So she saw a real fire, Mulder. It could have been anything—a bonfire . . ."

Mulder nodded agreeably. "That's what I thought at first," he said. "Until I remembered this . . ."

He stood and walked around his desk. He crossed the room to the television monitor on a metal stand in the corner. "A documentary I saw once—about an insane asylum." He turned on the monitor, then pressed the Play button. "It gave me nightmares."

Scully, still standing by Mulder's desk, crossed her arms and waited. "I didn't think anything gave you nightmares," she muttered.

Mulder shrugged. "I was just a kid."

The VCR engaged, and the blank screen of the monitor suddenly sprang to life.

The black-and-white image was unsettling: a close-up of a gaunt-faced man with a four-day growth of beard and cropped white hair. His cheeks were hollow. His skin sagged. The corners of his lips were drawn back in a demented grin. But the eyes were the worst of all. Set deep in their sockets, the flesh around them sunken and black, they revealed the man's naked, unadorned madness.

As the man spoke, Scully had to pull her attention away from his image in order to focus on his slurred voice.

"They took me away . . . the fire demons. The fire demons wanted their pound of flesh . . ."

On the monitor, the camera pulled back, revealing more of the man's surroundings. He was on a cot in a small, bare room, his legs held down by restraints. Scully noticed immediately that the man was missing one arm, but that his other arm was also securely tied down. The canvas straps that held him were worn, as if they'd been there for a long, long time.

"But I was too fast for them . . . I was too fast . . ."

Scully watched, both fascinated and repulsed.

"I was too fast," the man repeated, then broke into a scratchy cackle. He stopped laughing as quickly as he had begun, and his wild eyes paused for a moment, focused directly at the camera, directly at Scully. "Don't let them kill you. You can't let them kill you." The camera zoomed back in for a close-up. The man's face once again filled the screen, and Scully got the eerie impression that the man, somehow, across the years, was speaking directly to her. "You mustn't let them kill you. Or you'll never get to heaven. Do you hear me? You'll never get to heaven!"

Mulder reached forward and pressed a button on the VCR. The image on the screen froze, the man's mouth twisted somewhere between a sneer and a grimace.

"His name was Creighton Jones," Mulder said softly. "He pulled off the road on May 17, 1961. To take a nap. They found him three days later, so deranged by whatever he'd encountered that he had to be committed."

Mulder turned off the monitor and the VCR. The screen flickered, and then went black. He turned to face Scully.

"The state police found his car on I-40. Right in the middle of Dudley, Arkansas." Mulder allowed himself a small grin as he added, "The home of Chaco Chicken."

Scully didn't comment. It could be just a coincidence. There could be—in fact, there most likely was—a rational explanation.

Chapter Three

On the plane to Arkansas, Mulder immersed himself in the reference works he had brought with him, *Folklore and Legends of the Ozark Mountain People*, volumes one and two. When he shut the first volume to turn to the second, a small cloud of dust rose from the thick old book.

They landed at the decidedly low-tech Fayetteville Municipal Airport, picked up their bags, and made their way to the rental car desk. In a few minutes, they were on the interstate heading toward Dudley.

After about twenty minutes, Mulder, who had been scanning the fields, pointed out the window toward an open area and said, "There it is."

Scully, behind the wheel, glanced in the

direction Mulder was pointing. Even from the highway they could clearly see the burned patch of ground, a nearly perfect black circle, in the middle of the field.

Scully pulled off the highway at the next turnoff and followed the narrow country lane back to the field. When they drew opposite the scorched area, she parked the car.

The two agents got out of the car and began walking across the field toward the round black target. In spite of the sun in the cloud-speckled sky, the air was cold. Scully was glad that she was wearing her warm camel-hair coat. Mulder's lighter-weight overcoat flapped in the brisk wind, and Scully concealed a grin as she watched him pull the collar close around his neck. Well, she had told him it was going to be chilly.

They walked across the lush meadow until they reached the point at which the thick green grass abruptly stopped and the scorched black earth began.

Scully saw at once a thick layer of ash, along with dead embers and cinder fragments scattered throughout the circle. Clear evidence that this had been a wood fire. In spite of her partner's theory, she was quite certain this fire had been man-made.

And even this far from the highway, she noticed sadly, there was litter. A napkin fluttered feebly near the center of the circle, snagged on the jagged remains of a burned thistle. Mulder bent down and picked up a blackened plastic fork, warped by the heat of the fire into a twisted claw.

An indistinct shape sticking out of the earth on the other side of the circle caught Scully's eye. She walked over the ashy ground to get a closer look.

It was a branch that had been pounded into the earth, just on the green side of the borderline separating the scorched turf from the living grass. The branch had three limbs, reaching toward the sky like imploring arms. Scully had no idea what it was doing there—but she knew who would.

"Mulder," she said.

Mulder, still sifting through the ashes near

the center of the circle, turned and looked where Scully was staring. He stood and strode over to her side.

"What is this?" Scully asked.

"A witch's peg," Mulder answered. "It's supposed to ward off evil spirits."

"Can I help you folks?" a friendly voice called behind them.

Mulder and Scully both turned.

Approaching them from across the field was a uniformed man. As he got closer, they could see he wore a sheriff's badge on his fur-collared jacket. He seemed to be about forty, with a boyish face that was open and unguarded.

And he seemed sincerely interested in assisting them, giving them a bashful wave as he got closer. "Hi. I'm Sheriff Arens," he said simply, then gestured toward the highway. "I saw you back at the turnoff."

The two agents walked forward to meet him. "I'm Special Agent Mulder . . ." Mulder said, putting out his hand. The sheriff took it in his own and gave it a firm, reassuring shake as he flashed a warm smile. "And this is Agent Scully."

The sheriff gave her the same warm smile as he shook her hand. Scully returned his smile, realizing how much she missed this kind of simple genuineness—it was so rare back in D.C.

Mulder, meanwhile, reached into his overcoat pocket and pulled out his identification. "We're with the FBI," he said as he flipped open the black leather wallet and held it out for the sheriff's inspection.

Arens leaned forward to read the ID. He studied the badge, and then compared the photo to the man holding it. Mulder held it out until Arens was satisfied.

"Yep, you sure are," the sheriff said finally, nodding agreeably as he straightened up. "We don't see much of you fellas out here. What can I help you with?"

Scully spoke up. "We're investigating the disappearance of George Kearns."

The sheriff's eyebrows went up in surprise, but he nodded, saying, "Well, I'd be happy to help with whatever I can, but I'm not sure how much there is to investigate."

"Well," Mulder interjected—a little too sharply, Scully thought—"we can begin with his disappearance."

But the sheriff didn't seem to take offense at the tone. He just nodded again in agreement. "Sure," he said, quickly adding, "but there wasn't any evidence of criminal activity. Since no body turned up, we just went ahead and filed a missing-persons report."

The sheriff had just neatly summed up Scully's own feelings about the case. She turned to Mulder to see his reaction. It would be a shame if they had to head straight back to Washington—the idea of spending a few days enjoying a small town's hospitality appealed to her.

But apparently Mulder wasn't considering leaving town. In fact, he seemed to be on another wavelength altogether. He turned and pointed to the branch in the ground outside of the burn area.

"Why didn't you mention this witch's peg

in your report?" he asked the sheriff.

Sheriff Arens looked at Mulder, taken by surprise for the second time in as many minutes. He shifted his gaze to Scully. He cocked an eyebrow toward her, as if asking, "Is he serious?" Scully had to look away across the field. If Mulder was going to pursue this line of questioning, she thought, he's on his own.

"Because . . ." the sheriff began tentatively, "the fields around here are filled with 'em? I mean, a lot of these old hill people cling tight to their superstitions. I don't see any connection to George Kearns's disappearance."

Mulder indicated the charred circle. "What about this scorched area?" he asked.

"Illegal trash burning," the sheriff answered, seeming to be on firmer ground with this question. He chuckled. "I keep handing out citations, but they keep on doing it anyway. I suppose it's cheaper to pay the fine than haul it to the dump."

Mulder cut straight to the point. "Then you don't believe it's foxfire?" he asked.

"Foxfire?" Arens looked at Mulder. For a

frozen moment it seemed as if the sheriff was going to ask for another look at Mulder's FBI credentials, just to make sure he wasn't dealing with a lunatic impostor. "Sir, foxfire's nothing more than a ghost story about swamp gas."

Mulder just nodded, and Scully looked at him sympathetically. He never seemed to learn, she thought, or else he didn't care, that his farfetched theories were always rejected out of hand like this. She wished now that she had shown him the physical evidence for the wood fire before he had embarrassed himself.

But the sheriff was continuing. "Look, I don't know what you all are thinking, but George Kearns was just passing through this town ever since he got here."

Scully was intrigued by this observation. "How do you mean?" she asked.

"He never did fit in," the sheriff answered. "Not at the plant—not even in his own home." The sheriff caught himself, possibly wondering if he'd crossed over a line. But then he plunged ahead, lowering his voice. "It's no big secret that Kearns's marriage wasn't a happy one." Even though they were probably miles from any other living being, he spoke in a near whisper.

"Is that *all* you think happened here, Sheriff?" Scully asked. "That Kearns just decided to leave his wife? Without telling her?"

"I didn't know him that well, Ma'am. But from what I heard of him around town . . . let me just say it seems consistent with his temperament."

"Is that what his wife believes happened?" Mulder asked.

The sheriff shrugged. "Push come to shove, I'm sure she does. But you're welcome to ask her that yourself."

Scully looked to Mulder, and he nodded back at her. That was exactly what he was planning to do.

Chapter Four

The sheriff led the way through Dudley toward Doris Kearns's house. Mulder, in the passenger seat of their rented car, continued to muse as Scully drove, following the sheriff.

As soon as they had settled in their car, Scully had told him about the remains of the wood fire that she had noted. Mulder conceded that he, too, had seen the remains.

"But that indicates that some *person*, not a spirit, was responsible for the fire," Scully pointed out.

"I know," Mulder admitted.

"Then why on earth did you ask the sheriff about foxfire? And the witch's peg?" Scully demanded.

"I just wanted to see how open he was to

the possibility of a supernatural explanation," Mulder explained.

"And your conclusion?"

Mulder smiled wryly. "Not very."

Mulder knew he could be stubborn—he'd admit that freely. And it had paid off more often than not, whenever he found evidence for a theory he had faith in.

But he could also be objective. And right now he had to admit that his theory that a foxfire spirit was responsible for George Kearns's disappearance was fast becoming nothing more than, well, a will-o'-the-wisp.

Which put him back at square one, without even a glimmer of a theory to pursue.

Yet.

Objectively, there was a strong possibility that George Kearns had simply left town—just as the sheriff had suggested. In which case, after a brief interview with Mrs. Kearns, he and Scully would be on a return flight to Washington.

And there was always the possibility that Kearns *had* met his end, but under perfectly ordinary circumstances.

On the other hand . . . seeing the scorched earth in the field for himself only reinforced Mulder's feeling that there was a connection between Kearns's disappearance and Creighton Jones's horrifying experience back in 1961.

A connection that spanned three decades.

And if there was a connection, Mulder was determined to find it.

Scully continued to follow the sheriff's car through the town's small commercial district. The Chaco Chicken processing plant, outside of town, was the only large employer for miles around. Mulder noted that the few small businesses on Chaco Street provided only the meager essentials.

They quickly passed through what there was of the town and moved on to a spartan residential neighborhood. A few blocks later, the sheriff parked in front of an unassuming blue clapboard house. Scully pulled in behind him.

Sheriff Arens introduced the FBI agents to Doris Kearns, and Mulder gratefully accepted her offer of a cup of coffee.

Scully caught his eye—she knew this was out of the ordinary for him. Her face asked, silently, *What are you doing?* Mulder answered with a small, nearly invisible gesture of his own that she should go with Mrs. Kearns.

Scully headed toward the kitchen after Mrs. Kearns, saying, "Do you mind if I ask you a few questions?"

Sheriff Arens, with one quick glance toward Mulder, followed the women into the kitchen.

Mulder headed straight for the briefcase that he had noticed next to the couch while the introductions were taking place. Masculine in design, the leather scuffed and worn, the briefcase looked to Mulder to be Mr. Kearns's rather than his wife's. He ran his finger across the surface—the dust seemed to be consistent with ten weeks of accumulation.

As Doris Kearns leaned over the kitchen stove, Scully studied her carefully. She was probably in her mid-forties. Her eyes were nearly the same shade of blue as the paint on the clapboard shingles outside. And if she was worried about her missing husband, or upset by Scully's questions, she wasn't showing it.

"My husband and I had some issues that we couldn't work out," Mrs. Kearns said with little visible emotion. "I should have taken steps a long time ago. I talked to a lawyer once, but I couldn't go through with a divorce." She let out a short laugh that was one part bitterness and two parts relief. "I guess George saved me the trouble."

"Then you're fairly certain your husband left you?" Scully asked, trying to get a definitive statement.

Sheriff Arens leaned casually against the refrigerator, his thumbs hooked under his belt. He gave Mrs. Kearns a supportive nod.

"George left me a long time ago," Mrs. Kearns said flatly. "Right around the time I hit forty. Leaving town was just . . . a formality."

"Do you have any idea where he might be

now?" Scully asked.

"No. And I don't really *want* to know."

Mulder appeared in the doorway to the kitchen, reading from a sheaf of papers attached to a clipboard.

"Mrs. Kearns, this inspection report—your husband was getting ready to file it with the Department of Agriculture the day before he disappeared."

Mrs. Kearns forcefully shook her head. "I don't know anything about that."

Sheriff Arens, his face blandly curious, looked over Mulder's shoulder at the papers.

"You mean he never discussed his work with you?" Mulder asked.

"There were . . . I'm sure there were a lot of things he never discussed with me," she replied, sounding a bit flustered.

Mulder referred back to the papers. "Well, he cited several major health violations. He was about to recommend that the plant be shut down. That would have affected almost everyone in town."

"I told you—he never said a thing to me about what went on in that plant." The emotion in her voice had gone up a notch. Her eyes sought out Sheriff Arens's, and he offered her a sympathetic smile.

"I know this is difficult, Mrs. Kearns," Scully acknowledged, "but . . . do you know if your husband ever received any threatening phone calls, or anything unusual in the mail?"

"No. Never. Not that I know of. If he did, he didn't tell me."

Scully and Mulder exchanged glances. It was clear that Doris Kearns was near the breaking point, and they had to stop. Scully was sympathetic—this was a woman who had managed to come to grips with a husband who had abandoned her. To now suggest that someone might have had a motive to murder him was just too difficult for her to handle.

Mulder took a business card from his wallet and handed it to Mrs. Kearns.

"I'm going to give you my cell phone number. If your husband contacts you—or if anything else comes to mind—I want you to get in touch with me."

Mrs. Kearns took the card, nodding mutely.

Mulder turned to Arens. "Sheriff, if you don't mind, would you lead us to Chaco Chicken now?"

Sheriff Arens grinned. "You betcha."

Chapter Five

As a fully loaded truck moved out, an empty truck instantly pulled forward to the loading bay. Dozens of workers in white coveralls and hard hats emerged from the plant, pushing dollies stacked with plastic trays full of chicken—processed, packed, and ready to feed a hungry nation.

In a surprisingly short time the empty truck was loaded to capacity. As it trundled off, another empty truck, one in a seemingly endless line of trucks, pulled forward to take its place at the loading dock of the Chaco Chicken plant.

And above it all, as if floating serenely among the clouds, the face of Walter Chaco, painted on an enormous sign mounted on the factory roof, watched over all of the bustling activity. His painted smile beamed down on his workers. Next to his image, in proud letters twenty feet high, were the words CHACO CHICKEN. And beneath that, in smaller, but still huge, letters, the company motto: *Good People, Good Food.*

Two cars pulled up in front of the main factory doors and parked. Mulder and Scully got out of their car and sized up the place, wrinkling their noses at the nearly overpowering foul stench. They were joined by the sheriff, who seemed unaffected by the odor. *Was that an advantage, or a disadvantage, of living nearby?* Mulder wondered.

Together the three of them walked through the main entrance and into the plant.

As soon as Mulder and Scully entered the vast space of the processing plant's main floor, they were assaulted by the noise—the clanking, whirring, and hissing of machinery and knives. Next they noticed that the repulsive smells—spilled blood, internal organs, and waste—had actually intensified.

Then they saw it, the one inescapable fact of the plant. The chicken line. An unending, swiftly flowing stream of pale pink flesh marching past the workers in a limp-winged line-dance.

The chickens had already been slaughtered and plucked. As the carcasses entered the room, impaled on stainless-steel rods, one group of workers quickly sliced them open and removed the innards as they spilled out. The next group of workers lifted the gutted birds from the rods and hung them by their legs from metal hoops. The workers after them could then wash the carcasses inside and out.

The line moved fast. As the birds sped by, the workers, in a controlled frenzy, carried out their remorseless jobs of cutting, gutting, and spraying with incredible precision.

Mulder let out a low whistle. "So this is where chicken nuggets come from."

One man on the floor, wearing a blue business suit instead of the standard white coveralls, strode toward them.

"Sheriff, how can I help you?" he shouted over the din of the machinery.

"Hi, Jess!" Sheriff Arens returned the shout. The sheriff turned briefly to Mulder and Scully. "This is Jess Harold, the floor manager. Jess, these people are with the FBI."

Scully nodded. "We believe George Kearns's disappearance may have had something to do with a report he was going to file with the Department of Agriculture about this factory," she said.

Harold chuckled softly and shook his head, as though Scully had just told him a little joke. "You have to understand that ever since George got here, he'd been trying to shut us down."

Mulder glanced around the plant. It looked like excruciating, boring, repetitive work, but he couldn't see any obviously unsanitary conditions.

Scully persisted. "He cited multiple violations."

"I know he did," Harold said agreeably.

"Believe me, I've had to answer for every one of them."

"Was there any merit to his claims?"

Jess Harold smiled and said, "Let me show you something." He turned and walked briskly away. Mulder and Scully glanced at each other, then followed, with the sheriff right behind.

Sweat poured from Paula Gray's face. In her coveralls and hair net, with her face glistening and her breath coming in short ragged bursts, she bore little resemblance to the way she had looked that night in George Kearns's car.

She wasn't sweating because of her busy station on the chicken line. With a long ser-rated knife, she swiftly sliced open the next carcass that came her way, reached inside the body cavity with a gloved hand, and yanked out the bloody guts. Paula did this hundreds of times every day, and she was so used to it she never even broke a sweat. Usually.

And it wasn't because it was hot. The air in the plant was kept downright chilly. Still, her coveralls were damp and clung to her clammy skin.

And it wasn't because she was nervous. From where she stood, she had a clear view of the main door, but she hardly noticed when Sheriff Arens came in with the two strangers. She barely even registered her boss, Jess Harold, leading the sheriff and the other two down the line and toward the inspection station of the plant.

No, Paula had more important things to worry about—like keeping her mind focused on her work. Over the last few weeks it had become increasingly difficult to pay attention. On more than one occasion she had suddenly snapped back to reality after zoning out as two or three chickens passed by. The folks down the line couldn't keep covering for her—she had to shape up. Even though she was Walt Chaco's granddaughter, she would get no special favors from him. Nobody did. She had to prove herself worthy.

She had talked to the plant's doctor about what was happening to her—the headaches, the tremors. He had given her some bitter-tasting pills to help her with stress, but they weren't doing anything. She was considering seeing him again, when—

A sensation Paula had never felt before swept through her. A feeling of intense heat filled her body, and she began to shake, each tremor carrying with it its own special wave of pain. She clenched her teeth, and involuntarily tightened her grip around the wooden haft of the razor-sharp knife in her hand.

"Paula!" It was the co-worker standing beside her, a face she should have known. But suddenly nothing seemed familiar, everything was a threat. "Are you okay?" he asked.

The tremors inside her subsided as suddenly as they had begun. Paula took several deep breaths, and nodded. "I'm fine," she managed.

Her co-worker looked at her doubtfully, but returned to his post.

Still shaken, Paula reached forward and numbly slit open the next chicken coming down the line. And the next. Still breathing deeply, she forced herself to calmly slice each bird as it sped past. Inwardly, she tried to figure out what had just happened.

Something was definitely wrong with her. Slice, scoop.

She didn't want to admit it. Slice, scoop.

Her grandfather had said there was nothing to worry about. Slice—

Paula dropped her knife and screamed.

Instead of another chicken carcass jammed onto the next steel rod, George Kearns's head sat there, moving past her. His eyes bulged out of their sockets, staring up at her. His half-open lips quivered with the motion of the machinery. Blood dripped from the opening where his neck used to be.

Horrified beyond words, Paula reached out and wrested the decapitated head from the sharp steel spike that held it. Then she flung it as hard as she could, and watched it splatter against the packing-room wall. Staggering back, she turned and bolted from the room.

Leaving her co-workers to stare at what she had thrown. A chicken carcass, and nothing more.

"This is where George worked," Harold said to his visitors, gesturing around the clean, well-lit workspace. "Not a chicken leaves this plant without first passing through this inspection station."

Mulder and Scully nodded, watching the conveyor belt move past. After the chickens were processed in the big main room, and before they moved on to the packing area to be cut into pieces or bagged whole, the conveyor belt transported all the carcasses through this area. A team of inspectors stood next to the line, inspecting the body cavities and testing the joints of the carcasses as they sped by, jotting an occasional note on their clipboards.

"We've been operating this way for fifty years without any trouble from the USDA," Harold continued. "That is, until George came along."

As Mulder continued to look around the room, Scully faced Harold and asked flat out, "Did Kearns threaten to shut down the plant?"

"Oh, sure, he tried. But we have three other inspectors here who consistently give us top marks. Look," Harold said, reaching for a clipboard hanging on the wall. "This is our record. See for yourself."

He handed the clipboard to Scully. She flipped through the daily inspection forms, each one duly signed by one of the federal inspectors. Scully let her eyes wander down the grading grid on one of the forms. Only the boxes indicating the highest quality had been checked.

Harold shook his finger at the forms, his voice barely concealing his anger. "The only problem this plant ever had was George Kearns."

Scully lifted her eyes to meet his. "Was he problem enough to do something about?"

Harold seemed taken aback by the question. "If you're suggesting that someone may have actually done something to stop George . . ." Harold seemed to mull it over. "Well, I guess anything's possible. And George had a bone to pick with everyone." He looked pointedly at Scully. "Even the federal government."

Scully's face remained noncommittal. "What do you mean?"

"He filed a big worker's compensation claim," Harold replied smugly. "Said he was getting terrible headaches from the job. His lawyer called it 'line hypnosis.'"

"Yes, I've read about that," Scully said. "It's caused by high-speed, repetitive activity."

Jess Harold suddenly became defensive. "I won't deny that a lot of chickens pass through here every day," he said. "But we operate well within federal guidelines."

"What happened to his claim?"

Mr. Harold returned to his former smug stance. "It was dismissed. Actually, just a few weeks before George disappeared."

Mulder turned and gazed through an open doorway, back into the main area of the plant.

He watched as one worker went from gutting station to gutting station, pouring the waste that had collected there into a big plastic bucket. When it was filled, the worker strode to an industrial-size grinder, and poured the red contents of the bucket into the grinder's wide-open mouth. He flipped a switch, and the grinder roared. Mulder could see the pulpy contents spewing like a red lava flow down a chute and into a long metal trough mounted below.

He couldn't help wondering whether this was one of the health violations Kearns had noted.

"What's that?" Mulder asked Jess Harold, pointing toward the assembly.

"Oh, that," said Harold, leading them to the thumping and quaking piece of machinery that had caught Mulder's eye. "It's a feed grinder."

"*Feed* grinder?" Mulder asked.

Harold nodded. "It chops up bone, tissue—any part of the bird we can't package. We salvage the waste and use it as feed."

They all gathered around the feed grinder and looked at the bloody tissue inside. A giant metal screw spun, chewing up the flesh and bone and reducing it to a liquefied, slimy stew that poured into the lower trough.

Mulder made a face. "Chickens feed on chickens?" he asked, unable to hide his disgust.

"I know it doesn't sound too appetizing," Harold clucked, "but it's nutritious, and it cuts down on costs." He could see by their faces that he hadn't convinced them. "The meat is cooked and mixed with grain—there's no reason to let all that protein go to waste."

A buzzer sounded in the factory, and Jess Harold glanced at his watch.

"If you'll excuse me," he said, flashing an automatic smile, "I have to get ready for a shift change." Harold turned and walked away.

Scully looked at her partner. "Well, are you ready to admit we're on a fool's errand?"

Mulder didn't take his eyes off the feed grinder. "'If the fool would persist in his folly, he would become wise,' Scully." Then he winked at his partner. "William Blake."

Scully shook her head. "Even Blake would recognize a dead end when he saw one," she said as they turned and headed for the door. "I mean, whether George Kearns skipped town or somebody killed him, this case—if there *is* a case—can be handled by any agent from the Little Rock office." She grinned at Mulder. "Not you."

Mulder sighed. He couldn't argue with that. Sure, there were loose ends to Kearns's disappearance, but nothing Mulder could move forward on. His original theory had been shot down, and he didn't have a new one. He might have to admit that this time Scully—

A scream reverberated through the vast factory, tearing the thought from his mind. Mulder and Scully simultaneously spun around.

Halfway across the main floor, Paula Gray held her long, sharp gutting knife to Jess Harold's throat.

The two FBI agents stepped forward, sizing up the situation. Another scream erupted from the sidelines. The chicken line sped on, suddenly unattended.

The desperate young woman with the knife was edging backward toward the cutting tables, glancing wildly from side to side. Jess Harold, too frightened to resist, shuffled his feet awkwardly, walking backward alongside her, almost slipping in a puddle on the cement floor.

Mulder called out, "Let him go!" He reached for his gun. "We're federal agents!"

The other workers moved away from their stations. Some backed up against the walls; others cowered on the floor.

"Everyone stay calm!" Scully shouted, trying to head off a full-fledged panic or any ill-thought-out heroics that could endanger lives.

Scully took a few steps toward the crisis in the center of the room. From this distance, she could see the indentation that the pressure of the blade was making in Harold's neck—a tiny slip, a little more pressure, and the sharp knife would slice right through the frightened man's throat.

"Don't hurt him," Scully said in her calmest voice. "Just tell us what you want."

Paula's crazed eyes darted everywhere but at Scully. Scully wasn't even sure the girl knew she was there—something had literally frightened her out of her mind. Scully took two more steps forward, and Paula's eyes suddenly zeroed in on her.

Scully tried again, in her most calming voice, "*Please*, Miss, we can talk this thing out. We don't want anyone to get hurt."

Paula panicked, backing up three steps, pulling Harold back with her. He was starting to cry.

Mulder held his gun steady on the girl, and Scully was staying well clear of his line of fire. He couldn't risk a shot with the hostage so close, but he was prepared to fire if necessary. And Scully knew it.

"All right," said Scully, "I won't come any closer. I want you to trust me."

The young girl looked at Scully with an expression that, although still frightened, contained a glimmer of understanding.

Scully breathed a sigh of relief. Maybe this was going to turn out all right. "Why don't you give me the knife," she said.

Scully took another step closer. This time the girl didn't back off. Harold was blubbering like a baby.

Paula let Scully take yet another step toward her. The muscles in Paula's arms relaxed slightly, and the blade's pressure on Harold's neck lessened.

So the gunshot caught them all by surprise.

BANG! The sharp *crack* reverberated off the tile walls and echoed back and forth between the pieces of stainless-steel machinery.

An angry red hole appeared as if by magic in Paula's coveralls, directly over her heart. Without a sound, she began tumbling over sideways, her knife still against Jess Harold's neck.

Her dead weight pulled the knife down with enough force to neatly slice through Harold's skin. Under his Adam's apple, a bright red line blossomed. He reached frantically for the wound as Paula's body tumbled over the side of the trough and under the feed grinder, finally splashing into the bloody muck below.

Scully spun around and stared at Mulder, but he shrugged, bewildered—he hadn't fired his gun.

It was Sheriff Arens who gripped his weapon tightly in both hands, a tiny, telltale wisp of smoke rising from the barrel. Arens himself looked shocked by what he had just done.

Mulder ran to Jess Harold. Mulder practically had to pry the man's hands from the injury on his neck. He was relieved to see just a flesh wound—the knife had sliced through only the top layers of skin.

"Are you okay?" Mulder asked him.

But Jess Harold was still too shaken to answer.

Mulder passed him and moved to the side of the metal trough. He got just one look at Paula, her unseeing eyes staring up at him, before her body sank beneath the surface of the foul stew like a stone in quicksand.

Chapter Six

While they waited for the ambulance to arrive, Dr. Vance Randolph, the plant physician, wanted to take a look at Harold's wound. But Harold, holding a bloody handkerchief to his neck, just waved him away. Mulder used the time to get the dead girl's name and collect statements from the witnesses.

Scully looked across the room to where the sheriff stood. He was probably replaying the moment over and over again in his mind, Scully figured. Maybe he'd seen something she hadn't. Maybe she had only imagined that Paula was calming down.

When the paramedics arrived, Harold had regained enough composure to order one of his employees to drain the trough. As the thick, liquidy gruel slurped and gurgled through the pipe, Paula's body gradually became visible, resting at the bottom.

Once the paramedics had wheeled her body away and things had calmed down a bit, Harold finally allowed the doctor to examine and bandage the cut on his neck. Scully felt that Harold might be ready to answer a few questions, too.

And she was ready to ask them.

She began with a simple "Do you have any idea what might have prompted her attack?"

Harold shook his head. "None at all."

"No recent complaints or strange behavior?"

Harold shook his head more insistently, then winced at the pain the motion caused. "No. None. Paula was the brightest, most levelheaded person I had working for me. I can't even begin to imagine what might have brought this on."

Dr. Randolph, finishing the gauze bandage on Harold's neck, looked momentarily worried. Mulder noticed the look.

"What about you, Dr. Randolph?" Mulder asked him. "Do you have any ideas?"

Dr. Randolph gave the FBI agent a sharp look, but said nothing.

Harold finally broke the uncomfortable silence. "If you're through with me," he said as he stood up, "I've got a plant to get back on-line."

Without waiting for an answer, he strode off.

Dr. Randolph called after him, "Come by tomorrow and let me take a look at it—I'll make sure it's not infected."

Harold glanced back over his shoulder and nodded. "Sure." Then he headed toward his workers, who were still talking to each other in hushed whispers—and probably would be for some time to come.

Mulder and Scully looked at Dr. Randolph expectantly. The doctor cleared his throat.

"Paula came by last week," he began slowly, "complaining of persistent headaches. She said she'd been feeling irritable . . . and unable to sleep."

Scully asked, "Were you able to determine the cause?"

Dr. Randolph shook his head and said, almost apologetically, "I'm just the staff physician here. I don't usually treat anything more serious than minor cuts and scrapes. I'm, um, a little out of my depth when it comes to psychiatric matters."

"Then you found nothing physically wrong with her?" Scully pressed.

The doctor shrugged. "I sent her to County for a brain scan and an EEG. Both came back normal. So I assumed her condition was stress related."

Stress can make a person do a lot of things, Scully knew, even seize hostages. But it usually takes more than a week to get to that kind of breaking point. "Could it have been line hypnosis?" she asked.

"Like I said, I'm not qualified to make that diagnosis," the doctor said flatly.

Mulder leaned forward. "But you can tell us whether George Kearns came to you with similar complaints."

The doctor's eyes widened, and he nodded. "Why . . . yes. They both presented similar symptoms."

Scully asked, "How did you treat them?"

"I treated them both with pain medication—for the headaches. Codeine."

Scully nodded and turned to Mulder. "I think an autopsy on Paula Gray might help us clarify things."

Mulder was about to agree, when the doctor interjected, "I'm afraid I can't authorize that. You'll have to speak with Mr. Chaco."

"And why is that?" Mulder asked.

Dr. Randolph seemed surprised that they didn't know. "Because Walter Chaco is her grandfather—and her legal guardian."

Walter Chaco's mansion was exactly the kind of home that Scully imagined it would be. The house was nestled high on a hill overlooking the town, at the end of a long, tree-shaded drive. A row of white columns lined the front, lending the estate an old-fashioned but unfaded elegance. Scully could easily believe that a house like this one had been the inspiration for the Southern plantation in the film *Gone with the Wind*.

And this impression was only heightened by the palatial entryway to which Scully and Mulder were admitted when they rang the bell. They had little chance to appreciate the fine furnishings and appointments that stocked the main floor, however, because the maid whisked them quickly past it all. Still, Scully couldn't help noticing, as they passed through the enormous living room, a small room off to the side filled with primitive art and artifacts. They seemed so out of sync with the genteel Southern decor and architecture of the rest of the house.

The maid escorted them to the backyard, which was also of plantationlike dimensions. Scully could almost imagine that, if she squinted, she would be able to see hundreds of field hands hard at work in the distance.

But there was actually only one man working in the yard. He was not far from the house, tending to a few dozen prize chickens confined to a sturdy cage. His hair was gray edging toward white, matching his mustache. But the man was so fit, radiating such energy and strength, that Scully judged him to be less than sixty years old. Dressed in wrinkled, worn work clothes and holding a bucket, he tossed handful after handful of feed to the birds.

"Mr. Chaco?" Mulder asked respectfully.

The older man sighed, but didn't turn to face the two FBI agents. "Feeding these chickens," he said softly, "helps to clear my mind." He tossed another handful of the bird feed to the caged fowl.

"They're perfect creatures, you know," he continued. "We eat their meat, their eggs . . . sleep on pillows stuffed with their feathers." Another handful. "Not many people I know are as useful as these chickens."

This was always a hard moment for Scully. There was never a good time, a good way, to approach the next of kin with such a delicate request. All she could do was begin.

"We're sorry to disturb you, sir," she said. "We realize this is a difficult time for you."

She didn't have to continue, or to ask the unbearable question. Walter Chaco brought it up first as he turned to face her.

"You want to conduct an autopsy on my granddaughter?" he asked directly, his gray eyes steely and hard.

Scully nodded, and Chaco's eyes suddenly, surprisingly, softened. Moistened.

"Why?" he pleaded. "Do you think Paula had some kind of disease that made her act that way?"

He suddenly seemed like a vulnerable and weary old man, and Scully felt enormous sympathy for him. She wished she had a more definitive answer to give him, but she didn't. "We don't know," she said simply. "That's what we're hoping a postmortem will determine."

Then the steel edge, sharper than ever, came back to Mr. Chaco's eyes. "I thought your business here had to do with George Kearns," he snapped, scowling after he said the name, as though it had left a foul taste in his mouth.

Scully was taken aback by this abrupt change in his demeanor. This was no frail old man after all—she'd make sure to remember that. Meanwhile, Mulder had moved in to field the question.

"That's right," Mulder said, "but we suspect that Kearns's disappearance and what happened to your granddaughter might, in some way, be connected."

"How?" Chaco demanded.

"We're not sure yet," Mulder admitted, "but it's possible they both suffered from the same neurological disorder."

Walter Chaco looked from one FBI agent to the other, and then spoke to an invisible point between the two of them. "You know, when I came here after the war, Dudley was just a patch of dirt." He refocused his eyes, looking into the infinite distance, almost as though he were looking back into the past. "I built that plant and put my whole family to work there," he said. "We turned this town into one of the biggest chicken processors in the nation."

His speech had an almost hypnotic quality, Scully noticed. It wasn't so much the words. It had more to do with the energy, the passion, the very essence of the man himself. Scully had no trouble understanding how Chaco had become the richest, most influential person in town.

"We couldn't have had that sort of success with troublemakers and layabouts on staff."

"I assume," Scully said, "that you're referring to George Kearns."

Chaco looked at her sharply. "Men like George Kearns don't build things," he said, his voice cold. "They try to tear them down."

But is that a motive to kill him—or have him killed? Scully wondered. "Then you were aware of his recommendation to close down your plant?" she asked.

If Chaco knew what Scully was indirectly suggesting, he gave no sign of it. He bent down and gently lowered his now empty bucket to the ground. "You know," he sighed, "living a long life is a mixed blessing. You spend your youth trying to build something for yourself, your family, and your community." His face took on a bitter look. "Only to watch it all be torn away from you in your old age."

Even though she was trying to maintain an objective distance, Scully could feel herself being swayed toward Chaco's point of view. His powers of persuasion were profound—almost as if music were playing in the background as he spoke.

As Chaco turned to walk away, Scully realized he had not yet given them permission for the autopsy. She was about to call after him, but it was almost as though he had read her mind.

"You go do your autopsy on Paula," Chaco called to Scully, without looking back, as he climbed the back steps of his mansion. "I want to know what really happened to my granddaughter."

And with that he disappeared into the vastness of his house.

Chapter Seven

"I'm surprised he's not mayor," Scully said as they drove to the county building that housed the morgue.

"I'm surprised he's not *king*," Mulder said with a laugh.

Mulder dropped Scully off at the morgue and left to find what else he could about Paula Gray.

Scully got right to work, preparing the girl's body for the autopsy. Because it was Paula's erratic behavior that had led to her death, Scully decided that the first place to look for a cause was the dead girl's brain. And, as soon as she sawed open Paula Gray's skull, she knew she was on the right track. There was definitely something wrong with the brain—its texture just didn't look right.

Scully prepared a slide by placing a razor-thin slice of brain tissue on the narrow glass rectangle. She then peered at it through the microscope and carefully brought the image into focus. Instead of a uniform field of unbroken gray tissue, the material under the microscope was dotted with dozens of tiny holes.

Scully certainly hadn't known what to expect, but if she had been asked for a guess before examining the slide, this rare condition was about the last thing she would have predicted.

Mulder chose that moment to enter the lab, with a file folder in hand. He seemed ready to burst with excitement, but Scully spoke first as he came through the door.

"I think we've got something here, Mulder," she said, then guided him toward the microscope. "Take a look at this."

Instantly attentive, Mulder strode over to the microscope. "What am I looking at?" he asked as he bent forward to the eyepiece.

"It's a specimen from Paula Gray's brain," Scully answered.

Mulder paused for a millisecond halfway to the microscope, but then continued down to peer at the magnified tissue sample. He wasn't a trained pathologist like Scully, but even he knew that the irregular holes in the tissue didn't look good.

"What's wrong with it?" he asked.

"She had a rare, degenerative disorder called Creutzfeldt-Jakob disease," Scully answered.

Mulder slowly repeated the unfamiliar name after Scully, saying it just the way she had pronounced it: "*Kroyts-felt yah-kuhb.*"

Scully nodded. "It's characterized by the formation of spongelike holes in the brain tissue."

Mulder absorbed this. That definitely described what he was seeing through the microscope. He looked up at his partner.

"Why didn't this show up in any of her tests?" he asked.

Scully shook her head. "Short of an

autopsy, it's a very difficult disease to diagnose." She thought for a moment about her own limited knowledge of the condition. "Outside of a textbook, I've seen affected tissue only once—and that was back in medical school."

"Could this be the reason she attacked Jess Harold?" Mulder asked.

"Absolutely. Victims of Creutzfeldt-Jakob suffer from progressive dementia, violent seizures . . ."

Mulder glanced at Paula's body, which was laid out on an examination table not far from the microscope. In spite of the fact that the back of her head was missing, Paula's youthful face appeared surprisingly serene.

"Is it fatal?" he asked.

Again Scully confirmed the question with a nod. "This girl would have been dead in a matter of months."

Mulder walked over to the body and stared down at the pretty, young face—trying to make sense of what he saw there.

"Except that Paula Gray was no *girl*,"

Mulder said as he pulled some papers from the folder, and handed them to his partner. "This is her personnel file, Scully. Check it out."

Scully glanced down at the official-looking, typed personnel record in her hand. Mulder pointed to one particular entry, Paula's date of birth.

The date January 6, 1949, was neatly typed into the space.

"Nineteen *forty-nine?*" Scully couldn't help blurting, astonished.

Mulder nodded, and pointed at the corpse. "Which means that this *woman*, Chaco's granddaughter . . . was nearly *fifty* years old."

Scully reread the entry, and shook her head. "That's impossible. This must be a typo."

Mulder shrugged. "Then every date on that form—the year she finished school, the year she was hired—they would all have to be typos too."

Scully looked down at the woman on the examining table. "Mulder, it doesn't make any sense—it has to be some kind of mistake—"

"Let's go find out," Mulder said evenly. "Her birth certificate should be on file at the county courthouse." Then he grinned. "Who knows, Scully? This could turn out to be even more interesting than foxfire."

Chapter Eight

As they drove to the courthouse, Mulder had more questions about the oddly named disease Scully had detected in Paula Gray's brain. But first he had to remember the name.

"What was that disease again, Scully?" he asked. "Kramer-Yaddayadda?"

Scully smiled. "Creutzfeldt-Jakob."

"That's the one." Mulder smiled back, keeping his eyes on the road. "How likely is it that two people in town would have it?"

"Do you mean George Kearns?"

Mulder nodded. "He had the same, or similar, symptoms, right?"

But Scully shook her head. "It's an extremely rare condition, Mulder. The odds that Paula Gray and George Kearns both had it are astronomical."

"Couldn't she have caught it from him?"

But Scully shook her head. "It can be hereditary, but it's not contagious. That two unrelated people in the same small town would contract it is—"

Mulder looked over and caught her eye, supplying his own ending to her sentence: "—is a lot more likely than Paula Gray being three years shy of her fiftieth birthday."

Scully sighed. Paula Gray's age was a question they would be able to resolve in a few minutes' time, when they checked her birth certificate. Scully was fairly certain that they would find nothing unusual—just that there *had* been a mistake on the personnel form. But if it wasn't a mistake . . . well, she didn't even want to think about what that would imply until she had to. She turned her eyes back to the road.

Just in time.

"Mulder, look out!" she shouted.

Mulder snapped back to attention. A Chaco Chicken truck was barreling toward them—swerving back and forth, all over the narrow country lane.

Mulder had a split second to consider his options: There was a river next to the road on his left, and a line of trees on his right. On the narrow strip of road in between, he had precious little wiggle room to work with. If the truck even *nudged* the car on its way past, they would end up either wrapped around a tree trunk or sinking like a stone.

As the truck closed the distance down the middle of the road, Mulder yanked the wheel hard to the right. The car spun, heading toward the trees at a dizzying speed. The truck zoomed past on their left, leaving only inches of air between the two hurtling vehicles.

Mulder quickly veered away from the trees and held the wheel steady. Two of the car's tires were on the road while the other two rode the shoulder, bumping over the ground. Branches scraped the car windows and a huge tree trunk passed by so close, Scully feared for their lives. Finally Mulder managed to nose all four tires back onto the road surface and pull the car to a stop.

The Chaco truck was not so lucky. It raced off the left side of the road, flew over the embankment, and then, airborne, plunged ten feet into the river below. Water exploded in every direction.

Mulder and Scully jumped from their car. The deep tire tracks in the ground marked the point where the truck had left the road. As they crested the embankment, they could see the truck below them, cab down, in the murky water. A bumper sticker plastered to the rear of the truck, now sticking up in the air, read, HOW'S MY DRIVING?

"Call an ambulance!" Mulder shouted to Scully. He started scrambling down the embankment toward the cab of the crippled truck to reach the driver. But Scully was already dialing on her cell phone.

The bed of the truck was piled high with cages holding live chickens on their way to the Chaco plant. As Mulder crawled past, he could hear the panic-stricken clucking of hundreds of birds. Some of the lower containers were already under the red-stained, foul-smelling water, the birds presumably drowned.

The top of the cab was still above water level. The hood was crumpled back and the windshield was shattered, but if the driver had survived the crash, he could still be breathing in there.

Mulder crawled along the side of the truck, hanging on to the chicken containers to keep from slipping into the river below. *What is wrong with this water?* he couldn't help wondering as he glanced down. It looked red and thick, and the smell was almost unbearable.

Finally Mulder reached the cab, and he peeked in through the driver's window. His face fell. The truck driver apparently hadn't been wearing a seat belt. His body had shattered the windshield from the inside when the truck hit the water and came to its sudden and final stop.

The man was dead.

x x x

In just a few minutes the quiet stretch of county road was transformed into a cacophony of sirens and flashing lights. Squad cars, an ambulance, and a tow truck, along with a line of trucks from the processing plant, arrived on the scene. Leading the pack was Sheriff Arens.

As the men from the plant unloaded the chicken containers from the crippled vehicle and stacked them on the waiting trucks, the driver's broken body was removed from the cab and placed in the waiting ambulance. Finally, the tow-truck driver wrapped a heavy chain around the rear bumper of the half-submerged vehicle and began hauling it out of the water.

Mulder stood watching the activity as Scully, hanging up her cell phone, came over to him.

"I just got off the phone with Dr. Randolph, at the plant," she said quietly to Mulder. "He told me that this driver had the same symptoms as Paula Gray and George Kearns."

"So you think he's the third victim of Creutzfeldt-Jakob?" he asked, and Scully nodded. "But you just got through telling me that two cases in the same town would be statistically impossible."

"They would be . . ." Scully began. "Except . . ." She halted, then decided to continue. "I've come up with a sick theory, Mulder."

Was it her imagination, she wondered, or did Mulder's eyes actually twinkle? It was usually his department to come up with the bizarre theories, so he always seemed a little bit proud of her when she suggested one. This time was no exception. "Ooh," he said, taking her arm and leading her away from the nearby sheriff's deputies. "I'm listening."

After they had moved a little farther down the road, Scully began to outline her thoughts. "You remember that feed grinder at the plant? What if someone put Kearns's body in there?"

Mulder shook his head. He wasn't following her logic. "You said this thing's not contagious," he reminded her.

Scully explained, "You can't catch it like you'd catch a cold. It's not spread by a virus— it's a prion disease."

"Meaning?"

"It could have been passed to the chickens if they'd eaten some of the diseased tissue." She paused for a moment, and then made her point clear. "And then it could be passed on to anyone who ate *them*."

Mulder let that sink in. That *might* explain how three cases of a rare disease could pop up in this town. "Then anyone eating chickens from the Chaco plant would be at risk, right?" he asked.

Scully nodded. "It's possible. Sometimes, in England for example, cattle are incinerated to prevent them from passing mad-cow disease on to people."

Mulder shook his head. It was a good theory, but it wasn't going to work. "Scully, chickens from Dudley are shipped all over the country. If what you're suggesting is true, we'd be seeing an *epidemic*, not just a few isolated cases."

That's exactly what Scully was afraid of. She had even been ready to call the Centers for Disease Control to warn them. But Mulder was right—if the disease *was* being spread through the chickens, the nationwide epidemic would have already begun.

Mulder glanced over to see Sheriff Arens talking to the ambulance drivers. The ambulance was about ready to pull away, and the sheriff's work with them was nearly through.

"Sheriff?" Mulder called.

Arens headed over to where Mulder and Scully were standing.

"Yep?" Arens smiled at them, ready to be helpful, as always.

Mulder gestured to the river below them. The current was hardly flowing, and the stagnant red stream gave off a heady odor of filth.

"What's wrong with this water?" Mulder asked.

Arens glanced down at the river as though he'd never noticed a problem with it before.

"Oh, it's just runoff from the plant," he said with a smile. "Chicken litter, mostly. Some blood and parts from the birds."

A thought suddenly occurred to Mulder. "Was the river ever searched after Kearns disappeared?" he asked.

Sheriff Arens chuckled at that. "Are you kidding? Talk about a needle in a haystack." Arens laughed louder.

Mulder nodded and smiled along with Arens, allowing the sheriff to enjoy his laugh. Then, as the man settled down, Mulder said with finality, "I'd like the river dragged as soon as possible."

For once the sheriff's face lost its smile, replaced by a look of profound confusion. "Why would you want to do that?"

Mulder responded with what he thought was a reasonable answer. "To see what's in there."

Arens looked down at the water again, at last seeming to fully appreciate not only Mulder's seriousness but the river's condition.

"Well, listen," he said, "that's a filthy job, and I don't particularly care to do it—unless I know what you expect to find."

Mulder put his hands in his pockets, and said softly, "Nothing, I hope."

The sheriff didn't move. He didn't seem angry, or upset, or even argumentative anymore. He simply seemed frozen into immobility by a request that he couldn't compute. Maybe he thought that if he waited long enough, Mulder might just give up on this crazy talk and go away.

But Mulder stood his ground. "Look, Sheriff," he began, his voice barely masking his irritation with the sheriff's stubbornness. "If you don't want to handle this, I can get some of my men down here to do it."

The sheriff suddenly sprang back to life, the boyish grin snapping into place on his face. "I'll do it," he said, sounding surprisingly happy to be of service. "I just don't know why anybody would *want* to is all."

As the sheriff moved off to make the arrangements and requisition the necessary equipment, Scully moved closer to Mulder's side. She looked up at him with a questioning expression.

"It's just a hunch," Mulder said by way of explanation. "If Kearns didn't run off . . . if someone murdered him because of that inspection report . . . and if his body wasn't thrown in the feeding trough . . . then it has to be somewhere."

He looked down at the deep-red opaque water below. This seemed a fine place to lose a body.

Sheriff Arens was as good as his word.

He transmitted a request to the county Water Management Board, and within an hour the spillway upstream was closed. The water level in the river dropped almost immediately. By that time a number of deputies were already deployed on the river in inflatable rafts, dredging the bottom with long, wide nets.

Mulder, Scully, and Arens watched from the bank. Mulder seemed especially nervous, pacing back and forth. He wondered if, after raising such a fuss, he really was just wasting everybody's time.

"Hey, we've got something!" A cry rang out on the river. The deputies in one of the rafts were hauling up their net. One of the men turned and waved at Arens and the FBI agents. The other deputies pulled the net the rest of the way out of the river and dropped it onto the floor of the raft. Then the deputies began paddling the raft toward the short, old wooden pier jutting into the water.

"Did they find Kearns?" Mulder wondered aloud.

"Let's go see," the sheriff said, and the three of them walked over to the pier.

They walked out onto the pier. As it creaked and shifted under their feet, Mulder worried that the aged wooden structure wouldn't be able to support their weight. He quickly put those concerns aside as Arens's deputies raised the net from their raft and deposited it on the end of the stubby dock.

The net was filled with bones, dripping wet and glistening in the sun. This should have been a moment of minor triumph for Mulder. But there was a problem.

The net was *literally* filled with bones. There were simply far too many to have come from only one person. Just at a glance, Mulder counted the bones from at least five human legs.

If the remains of George Kearns were in the river, he obviously had company.

Chapter Nine

The deputies spent the rest of the afternoon dragging the river, and they hauled up several more nets full of bones as the day progressed.

As they were brought up, the bones were immediately transported to the county morgue and dumped unceremoniously in the middle of the forensics-lab floor. In a short time the pile had grown into a grisly mound. Scully spent the afternoon sorting through the bones, separating them into individual bodies.

Mulder divided his time between the river and the lab. As he reentered the lab, he saw Scully sitting by one small pile of bones on the floor. In front of her was a partial rib cage, part of a pelvis, and a forearm. Scully was holding a femur, the large bone in the thigh, and examining it through a square magnifying glass.

"Sheriff Arens is outside with more," Mulder announced. "And when we left, they were still pulling bones from the river."

Scully nodded. This was going to be a long, long night. "Well, so far," she said, looking up at Mulder as he crouched next to her, "I've been able to isolate nine distinct skeletons." She pointed at the one she was sitting next to. "This one belonged to the late George Kearns."

"Really?" asked Mulder, impressed. "How can you tell?"

Scully held out the femur for Mulder's inspection. A thin steel rod protruded from the bone, near a hairline crack. "This pin in his femur. According to his medical file, Kearns broke his right leg four years ago."

Mulder looked around the room at the neatly organized, partially reconstructed skeletons. The recovered dead. He noticed that, of all the bones that had been found on the bottom of the river, there were no skulls among them. "What about the others?" he asked.

"Well," Scully sighed. "I'll need more sophisticated equipment to be certain—but I estimate that some of these bones could be as much as thirty years old."

Mulder studied his partner's face. This was a remarkable finding. But Scully had more to reveal.

"And all of them share one strange detail," she said.

Mulder mentioned the one thing that he had noticed: "They all seem to have lost their heads."

"Yes, but besides that . . ." Scully pointed to a nearby pile. "The older bones show signs of decay and surface abrasion, just as you'd expect . . ."

Mulder nodded. Then Scully picked up George Kearns's femur again and handed it to Mulder. "But for some reason," she said, "all the bones—even Kearns's—are smooth and buffed at the ends."

Mulder examined the femur. The normal, rough brown surface of the bone gave way to a shiny, rounded end.

"It's almost like they've been polished," he said.

Scully shrugged, and said uncertainly, "It could just be erosion from the water, but—"

"But that water hardly had any current," said Mulder, finishing the thought. "Besides, this level of erosion wouldn't be confined to just the ends of the bones."

Scully studied her partner. "Any theories?" she asked as Mulder handed back the bone.

Mulder did have the faintest glimmer of an idea. There was one possible explanation that occurred to him for the condition of the bones. But before he could verbalize the thought, even to Scully, he needed to check something out. He pulled his cell phone from his pocket and punched in a number.

"Maybe," he said softly, disturbed by his own train of thought, as the phone on the other end started to ring.

Even more interesting than foxfire, he thought now. *Oh, yeah . . . way more interesting . . .*

In the hallway outside the morgue, Sheriff Arens poured himself a cup of coffee. Or at least tried to.

It wouldn't take a trained observer to see that he had been affected by the day's events. His hands shook and the coffee splattered over the countertop. Arens had to force himself to put down the glass pot gently. His customary pleasant expression was more strained than ever as he began to clean up the mess.

The last person he wanted to see at that moment was Doris Kearns. She came rushing into the room, fear and anguish vivid on her face.

Arens took a step toward her. "Doris . . ." he began.

She stopped a few steps away. Her eyes were huge, unblinking.

"Is it true?" she asked. Arens didn't answer at first, searching for the right words. "Just tell me!" she pleaded.

Arens put his hands up. "Doris, I want you to listen to me—"

But Doris wouldn't. She could read, instinctively, what his response meant. "They found him, didn't they?" Her voice was flat—she sounded like she was already in shock.

Sheriff Arens stalled for another moment. "We brought up quite a few remains at the river this afternoon, and . . ." Arens let out a heavy sigh. He could stall no longer. "George's were among them."

Doris started to cry, and shake her head, as she backed away from the sheriff.

"No . . ." she whimpered.

"I'm sorry, Doris," Arens said. Doris's whimper turned into a wail.

"No!" she screamed. Then she turned and ran.

"Doris!" Arens called after her. "Don't worry—we'll take care of you! Doris! . . ."

But his voice trailed off as she raced around the corner and out of sight.

The sheriff's face fell, and his eyes got even sadder. What was happening to their town?

The bandage was really starting to get on his nerves.

Every time Jess Harold nodded, every time he shifted position, every time he put a phone to his ear or turned his head, it scratched and pulled and tugged on his skin. It was driving him crazy. Harold was just about *this close* to ripping it off his neck.

Instead, he settled for scratching around the edge of the white gauze square, and he yanked once again at his collar.

While he was on duty at the plant, it actually didn't bother him that much. There was so much activity going on, so many things he was responsible for, that he didn't have time to let it get to him.

It was when he was alone, when it was quiet. That was when the bandage started to remind him about what Paula had done to him. That was when he let himself begin to wonder why.

Like right now, for instance, sitting in Dr. Randolph's office, waiting for the doctor to see him.

The day-shift workers at the plant had gone home. Harold had overseen the shift change, and would have left himself, except for the scrawled note he had received from Dr. Randolph. It said the doctor wanted to see him—and that it was urgent.

When Dr. Randolph finally stepped into the small room, the look in his eyes confirmed what Harold already knew.

"I get the feeling I'm not here so you can check on my neck," Harold said dryly.

Dr. Randolph was in no mood for ironic banter. "They found bones in the river," he said, in a hushed, frightened voice.

A heartbeat passed, and then Harold nodded. "I know. I heard," he said casually.

Harold's calm attitude seemed to agitate the doctor. "Did you also hear that Clayton Walsh has come down with the symptoms?" he asked, his quivering voice rising ever so slightly.

Harold looked up at him sharply. Walsh was a worker on the line. A good man. Young, with a wife and little daughter. No, he *hadn't* heard.

"That makes four," the doctor continued. "It's getting worse with every day that goes by."

Harold had to acknowledge that the doctor's concerns had merit—that perhaps the man wasn't overreacting after all. Maybe, Harold realized, he himself was the one who hadn't been aware of the true scope of the problem.

"Somebody has to tell Mr. Chaco," Harold said finally.

"He *knows* what's happening," the doctor responded. "He's just not *doing* anything about it."

"Maybe I could talk to him . . ." Harold thought aloud.

"You can try," Dr. Randolph snapped.

Harold stood. Even if what the doctor was saying was true, the man was making him nervous, and he wanted to get out of there. "Yes. I'll talk to him. He'll listen to me," he said as he headed for the exit.

Dr. Randolph was silent until Harold reached the door. "And if he doesn't?" he finally blurted out.

Jess Harold turned to look back at the trembling doctor. He seemed to be on the verge of tears. Harold knew that Dr. Randolph was anxious and upset.

But was that all?

Harold briefly wondered if it would be possible for the doctor to detect the symptoms of this disease in himself.

Not knowing the answer, and not willing to pose the question, Harold turned and walked out the door.

Chapter Ten

It was twilight, and the streetlights in town were turning on one by one.

It *had* been a long afternoon in the morgue sorting through bones, and the job still wasn't done. But one did work up an appetite.

So Scully drove through the town's small commercial center, scanning the signs on fast-food restaurants for something worth eating. As she'd suspected, most of the places served only chicken.

When in Rome . . . She smiled to herself, and pulled into the parking lot of Sweeney's Fried Chicken.

Twenty minutes later she was back at the morgue, clutching the warm bucket of fried chicken under her arm as she walked into the building. As she came through the door, she saw Mulder hunched over the fax machine, poring over pages that were still coming in.

"I ran a check of all missing persons last seen within a two-hundred-mile radius of Dudley," he explained. "In the last fifty years, eighty-seven people have disappeared near here."

He handed Scully the pages of the fax he had received so far. The top page contained a map of Seth County, Arkansas, with Dudley at the center. Numbered black dots, each representing a missing person, studded the map. Most of the dots were clustered in and around Dudley. The supporting pages contained the corresponding list of the names and the dates of the disappearances. More pages were still rolling out of the fax machine.

Scully simply stared at the pages in her hand, stunned by the magnitude of the crime they were investigating.

"Judging from the forensic evidence," Mulder said, looking down at the piles of bones that covered the floor, "I'd say the same person or persons were responsible."

Scully followed Mulder as he made his way through the skeletal jigsaw puzzle before them. A pile of unsorted bones lay in the middle of the room, surrounded by nine carefully arranged partial skeletons. She had thought nine bodies were a lot—but apparently they had retrieved only the tip of the iceberg.

She tried to make some kind of sense of this new information. "It may have been the work of some kind of a cult," she said slowly.

Mulder nodded. "Scully, I checked out an idea, and . . ." He crouched down by one of the piles. "Look at these bones," he said, picking one up and examining it himself. "You said they looked polished at both ends. Well, one possible explanation is they were boiled in a pot."

"*Boiled?*" Scully asked, confused. "Why would they be boiled?"

Mulder looked up at his partner, and explained, "Anthropologists used similar evidence to prove cannibalism among the

Anasazi tribe of New Mexico."

"Cannibalism? What does that have to do with . . ." Her voice trailed off.

Mulder shifted his gaze to the fried-chicken bucket under Scully's arm. "Scully," he said, "I think that the good people of Dudley may have been eating . . ." He paused, and swallowed hard before he went on. "A lot more than chicken."

Scully stared at her partner in disbelief, then looked back at the bones scattered around them. "You think these people were . . . *eaten?*" she asked. It was not easy to shock her, but this did it.

Scully started to let Mulder's suggestion sink in. Her stomach began to feel queasy, and her knees went weak. She realized that her theory—that people were getting ill from eating tainted chickens—was too complicated. There was a simpler, more direct, and much sicker explanation.

"Well, then," Scully said, suddenly sitting so she wouldn't lose her balance from an onset of dizziness, "Paula Gray may have contracted Creutzfeldt-Jakob . . . from *eating* George Kearns." There. She'd said it.

Mulder nodded again, his mouth a grim line.

Scully glanced down at the bucket of fried chicken in her arms—she had suddenly lost her appetite. *Who was involved?* she wondered. *How far did this thing go?*

"And that could also begin to explain Paula's youthful appearance," Mulder added, almost as an afterthought.

Scully was still reeling over the possibility that a group of outwardly normal, seemingly well-adjusted people were making a habit of eating other people. But Mulder's last statement didn't make any sense to her at all.

"What are you talking about?" she asked. "*What* explains her appearance?"

"Some cannibalistic rituals," Mulder answered, "are enacted with the belief that they can prolong life."

Scully shook her head decisively. "Cannibalism is one thing, Mulder," she said, "but increasing longevity by consuming human flesh—"

"People believe it, Scully. From ancient to fairly modern times, in the mythology of many different cultures, the reward for eating human flesh is eternal life."

Scully stood up. The wave of nausea had passed. Now that they were on to purely speculative matters, she felt more like herself. She didn't even have to verbalize the skepticism on her face.

"I'm not saying it really works," Mulder insisted, then paused. "But we both saw Paula Gray."

"We never confirmed the date of birth in her personnel file," Scully reminded him.

"Then the records in the courthouse should tell us how old she really was," Mulder said. Then he grinned at Scully. "And," he went on, "if anyone else in Dudley is lying about their age."

Mulder grabbed his jacket and headed for the door. Scully sighed, put down the bucket of chicken, and followed.

Chapter Eleven

Jess Harold had the distinct impression that he was not getting through to Walter Chaco.

They stood close together in the room of Chaco's mansion where Chaco kept all of his souvenirs from his days in the South Seas. Mr. Chaco referred to this room affectionately, and with some accuracy, as his museum. Every piece in the collection had a long and detailed history, some of which he had taken the trouble to type up in abbreviated form on tiny cards next to the items on display.

Chaco was so attached to his treasures that whenever he stood among these prized pieces of history, he almost seemed to lose himself in the past.

Even now Chaco stood in silent reverie

before a magnificently carved mahogany cabinet. Having flung the ornate doors wide open, he was admiring its contents. Jess Harold wasn't sure if Chaco had heard a word of his concerns.

Finally, with a deep sigh, Chaco swung the heavy doors shut. As he closed the wooden hasp, securing it with a small steel padlock, Harold tried again.

"You've got to do something about what's happening, Mr. Chaco," Harold said, his voice full of urgency. "People are getting scared. They don't know what to make of things."

Chaco turned to Harold at last, his voice deep and strong. "They're losing their faith," he said, sounding rather like a father speaking to a disobedient child.

Harold spoke softly. "It's hard to hold on to, the way things are going," he said. These weren't easy words to say, especially to Mr. Chaco of all people. Harold had expected some kind of reaction. Maybe even an explosion. But Chaco said nothing. He suddenly looked old and defeated. *Maybe*, Harold thought, *maybe Dr. Randolph was right about Chaco.*

Harold was overcome by a feeling close to dread. What if, after all these years of trusting him, believing in him and his ways, there was nothing that Mr. Chaco could do about the sickness after all? What if they were all doomed?

"Three more have gotten sick since yesterday!" Harold said, his voice raised in anger to Walter Chaco for the first time.

Chaco reacted then. "I lost my granddaughter in this!" he shouted back, his temper flaring. "So don't tell me what we're up against!"

Chaco turned away from Harold and tried to get himself under control. *Accusations and counteraccusations will do no good now,* he thought. They had to work together, like a family should. He spoke again, more tenderly. "I said I'd handle it."

But Harold wasn't satisfied. "I know that's what you said, Mr. Chaco—but how?"

If Chaco had an answer, the sound of the

doorbell ringing stopped him from supplying it.

Chaco and Harold looked at each other, each wondering who it could be. Perhaps the FBI agents.

But when the maid opened the front door, they were relieved to see only Doris Kearns.

Chaco stepped forward to greet her, his face crinkling into a warm, fatherly smile.

"Doris," he said. Then, looking closer at her red, puffy eyes, he asked, "Have you been crying?"

She looked up at him and nodded. "I can't do this anymore, Mr. Chaco," she said. She was trying to put on a brave face, but before she knew it, she started to sob again. "I can't keep lying," she managed to get out.

Chaco put his hands on her shoulders. "It's all right, Doris," he said. His voice was warm. It was deep and comforting. Just hearing him say her name made Doris feel better. "Jess told me what happened," he continued, nodding his head toward Jess Harold, who had stepped into the light. "You have nothing to worry about," Chaco concluded, smiling.

"But," Doris began tentatively, "won't they think I did it?"

"No," Chaco said, as though he'd never heard such a farfetched notion. "They won't think any such thing."

Doris started to sob again. "But . . . I *did*," she said, breaking down. "I helped . . ."

"George was no good, Doris," Chaco said soothingly. "He didn't fit in here—you knew that."

"But he was my husband."

Chaco nodded, but his expression was stern. "That was the price you had to pay," he said. His voice was gentle, but with an unmistakable, reassuring strength behind the words. "You knew that from the beginning."

"But those FBI agents—"

Chaco looked down into her eyes and spoke with all the conviction that was within him. "This town wasn't built in a day, Doris. It's not about to fall apart in a day." Doris nodded, reassured in spite of herself. "You're a part of us now," he went on, his voice melodious and full, "and we're going to take good care of you."

Chaco gently guided her back to the front door. "Now I want you to go home and get some rest," he advised her. "This whole thing will blow over soon enough, and you'll wonder what all the fuss was about."

Doris believed him. She even smiled. Of course he was right. She was already beginning to wonder why she had gotten so upset.

"I'm sorry," she said. How could she have ever doubted him? Doris felt suddenly shy, embarrassed. Would Mr. Chaco ever forgive her for her doubts? She looked up into his face—yes, she could see he had already forgiven her. He was smiling down at her, like a father to a beloved daughter.

"That's all right," he said soothingly. "We all understand." His words were simple, yet so full of meaning. So full of blessed relief from her doubts and fears. "Good night," he said.

Doris turned to go. She had been privileged to receive Mr. Chaco's blessing. As she walked out the front door and into the night, her step felt lighter than it had in days.

Inside Chaco's "museum," Jess Harold was beginning to see things differently. He knew the power of Chaco's voice, the skill with which he used it. And he was afraid the power was faltering, along with the man behind it.

Chaco walked back to Harold. "She'll be fine," he said reassuringly.

Harold looked at the closed front door. He felt more at liberty to speak his mind in front of Chaco than he ever had before. "She's not stable," Harold said pointedly.

Chaco looked at him sternly. "She's one of us now," Chaco said sharply. "One of our family. Part of our town."

Harold looked at Chaco and spoke back just as sharply. "Unless we do something about her, there won't be any town left to speak of."

As Harold began walking to the door, he heard Mr. Chaco say simply, "No."

Harold felt compelled to stop, much as if

Chaco had actually laid a hand on him. The man still had the power in him, Harold could see, with a mixture of both fear and relief.

"Once we start turning on ourselves," Chaco continued, "we're no better than animals."

Harold nodded. Chaco was making sense to him now. The townspeople of Dudley were a family. It had always been that way.

"It's the FBI we should be worrying about," Chaco said slowly as the thoughts formed in his mind. "They're the real problem . . ."

Harold looked at him. Of course—it was so simple. All they had to do was get rid of the outsiders, and things would go back to normal. He liked the sound of that very much.

The only question was, how?

For the first part of her drive home, Doris Kearns felt much better. Mr. Chaco's words were so reassuring, his tone so convincing. All would soon be well, just like he'd said.

But as the miles rolled by, her old doubts

began to resurface. What if the FBI agents came to question her again? How would she be able to answer them? How would she hold up? Mr. Chaco hadn't really addressed that. He hadn't told her what to say.

By the time she had reached home, she was frantic again. She was not only filled with the old fears, but with some new ones as well. She searched her memory for a trace of the comfort and relief she had been feeling only moments before. She thought back over Mr. Chaco's actual words.

"There's a price to pay," he had said. And, "We're going to take care of you." Those weren't necessarily comforting thoughts. What if there was hidden meaning in his words? Maybe they were really going to take care of her—for good!

She ran inside the house, going straight to the kitchen. Stuck by a magnet to the refrigerator door was a card she had placed there the day before.

She looked at the card for the number, and the man's name.

Fox Mulder.

By the time Mulder and Scully arrived at the
county courthouse, it was well after dark. The
building was closed for the night and most of
the workers had gone home.

But the door was still unlocked.

Small towns can be so trusting, Mulder
thought as he and Scully slipped inside. After
checking the directory, they quietly made
their way up the dark staircase to the hall of
records, on the second floor.

The Hall of Records. A lofty name for
spartan rooms filled with metal file cabinets.
It was the place where all the official documents of the town were gathered. Deeds,
marriage licenses, birth and death certificates—with enough time in this place, one
could assemble a complete chronological
history of the life of this town.

Mulder and Scully stopped in front of a
door marked BIRTH REGISTRATION, the room
where the birth certificates of everyone born
in the town were carefully preserved.

Or, at least, used to be.

As soon as they saw the door ajar, they knew something was wrong. And when Mulder pushed it open, they could both smell an unmistakable trace of smoke.

Scully flicked the light switch, but nothing happened. They both snapped on their flashlights, and immediately saw the rows of blackened file cabinets lining the walls. Some of the drawers were hanging open, revealing piles of gray ashes—all that remained of the townspeople's birth certificates.

"Somebody's been playing with matches," Mulder quipped.

"It smells like a *recent* fire," Scully added, sniffing the air in the room.

"I bet it's no coincidence that it hit only the birth records," Mulder said. "I guess someone was expecting us." He tried to remember who, if anyone, had been near enough to overhear them when he and Scully had discussed visiting the Hall of Records.

His cell phone rang, interrupting his thoughts. He retrieved it and flipped it open.

"Mulder," he said into the receiver.

"It's Doris Kearns," said the frightened woman on the other end, her voice trembling. "I'm at my house. I need to speak with you right away."

"Are you all right?" he asked.

"I'm afraid for my life," she said. Mulder heard what sounded like an involuntary sob, then, "I'm afraid he'll kill me."

"Who?" asked Mulder.

He heard the heavy breathing on the other end of the line as a decision was being made. Finally the answer came.

"Mr. Chaco," Doris Kearns said, breaking down.

That was all Mulder needed. "All right, Mrs. Kearns," he said into the phone. "I want you to stay in the house and lock the door—and don't answer the door until Agent Scully gets there."

"All right," the sobbing woman on the other end said. Mulder heard the click as she hung up her phone.

Scully looked at Mulder questioningly as he slipped the phone back into his pocket. It sounded like he had just volunteered her services to go pick up Mrs. Kearns. That left only one question.

"Where are *you* going?" Scully asked him.

"To take Chaco into custody," Mulder answered.

As soon as Doris Kearns placed the phone down in its cradle, she ran to the front door to check it. Since she had run into the house so quickly, with so much on her mind, she could not remember if she had locked the door or not.

She was surprised to find the front door not only unlocked, but slightly open. She looked at it fearfully—she didn't remember leaving it like that. But then she had run for the kitchen so quickly, so intent on calling the FBI, maybe it was possible that she hadn't closed it all the way.

As she pushed the door closed and turned

the latch, all the lights in her house went out.

"No!" she cried, turning around. Someone else was inside the house—someone who had just thrown the circuit breaker.

Shaking, Doris moved across the dark entryway. She tried to keep thinking straight—if she could just make it to the phone. She took a few more steps, when—

A giant figure with a hideous face stepped from the living room and stood directly in her path. She recognized who it was at once, from the one ceremony she had attended. He was wearing the tribal mask. Red feathers fringed the edge. Yellow streaks of paint crossed its cheeks. Even in the darkness of the house, Doris could see the glowing white outline around the eyes and mouth of the mask.

Then she saw the ceremonial ax in the masked man's hands. She knew he was there for only one reason.

"No!" she screamed. "Please!"

But the masked figure stalked closer. Doris

took a step back, and then another, and then she felt the front door, locked and latched, at her back.

She screamed again as the man advanced toward her. She had no time to turn and fumble with the door. The man in the mask was towering directly above her. As he raised the ugly iron blade over her head, she finally passed out.

Chapter Twelve

As soon as Scully pulled up to Doris Kearns's house, she knew something was wrong.

The house was completely dark.

In Scully's experience, people who believed themselves to be in danger rarely sat alone in the dark. In fact, they generally kept every light in the house blazing until help arrived. A dark house was not a good sign.

She parked her car in the driveway behind Doris Kearns's car, hurried to the front door, and rang the bell.

No one answered.

Scully aimed her flashlight through the window of the front door. She could make out the size and shadows of the entryway, but saw nothing moving inside.

"Mrs. Kearns?" she shouted hopefully. "It's

Agent Scully." There was still no response. She tried the door, but it was locked.

Scully walked around the side of the house, the wind whipping her overcoat around her. She kept the flashlight trained on the flagstone path and made her way to the back door.

It opened when she turned the knob.

Scully drew her gun and gingerly stepped in through the open door.

She found herself entering a service porch—her flashlight revealed a washing machine and dryer, a closed cabinet that she presumed was a pantry. An open doorway to her left led to the kitchen.

"Mrs. Kearns?" Scully said again. The only answer was the rushing wind outside and the branches scraping against the side of the house.

Scully went through the doorway into the kitchen. She played the beam of her flashlight around the room. There were no signs of a struggle, no sign of anything amiss. She walked on through the kitchen, toward the entrance that led to the central hall and the rest of the house.

With a rush of air the back door slammed shut behind her. Scully spun around, pointing her gun and flashlight at the door. No one was there. She scanned the area again with her flashlight until she was satisfied.

Only the wind, she thought, turning back toward the hallway.

She was determined to search the rest of the house, even though she already suspected that she wasn't going to find Doris there.

As Scully searched through Doris Kearns's house, Mulder arrived at the Chaco mansion.

Half a minute after he'd rung the bell for a second time, Mulder began to seriously consider forcing his way inside. Then the front door finally swung open.

The maid stood there, her face grim.

Mulder held up his FBI identification. "Is Mr. Chaco in?" he asked firmly.

The maid backed up, allowing Mulder

into the entryway. "I'll see if he's still awake," she said.

As she disappeared up the stairs, Mulder quickly walked straight toward Chaco's "museum." The walls were filled with ornate masks and drums, but it was the glass display case that immediately caught his eye.

It held a human skull. And bones that had been carved into tools.

Mulder moved closer to study the items in the case. On the top shelf were photographs of a younger Chaco. In one shot, Chaco sat in the cockpit of a World War II–vintage military plane. In another photo, Chaco was standing in a jungle clearing with the members of an apparently primitive tribe. Chaco, in his army uniform, appeared in sharp contrast to his tribesmen companions, who wore only necklaces and loin-cloths. The dark-skinned men stood proud, their nearly naked bodies painted with bright colors, long spears in their hands. Mulder examined the picture even more closely. Although it was hard to be sure, it looked like the necklaces the men wore were made of *teeth*. Human teeth.

Mulder glanced at the other items in the case. The pieces of the puzzle were falling into place. The bones that were carved into functional objects were of human origin. The skull was surrounded by a fringe of white chicken feathers. Mulder read the legend that had been neatly typed onto a card that was propped up next to the skull: JALE TRIBE, NEW GUINEA, 1944.

Oh yes, Mulder had heard of the Jale. They were long suspected by anthropologists of engaging in cannibalistic practices. Such suspicions had never been proven. *Until now*, Mulder thought.

He turned from the glass display case and saw the rich, red carved mahogany cabinet that dominated the small room. Mulder crossed to it and examined the wooden hasp and padlock that kept it shut. *Too bad these doors aren't made of glass*, he thought. Judging from the size and prominence of the chest—and the weight of the padlock—he concluded that whatever was inside must be pretty important.

He turned when he heard the maid's footsteps on the stairs. She reached the bottom and looked around the foyer, puzzled. Then she saw him standing in the small chamber, and her expression became, if anything, even tighter.

"I'm sorry," she said, trying to force a smile, "but Mr. Chaco is unable to see you now."

Mulder nodded, letting it pass. He jerked his thumb back toward the cabinet. "Do you know what's in there?" he asked.

The maid looked stricken. The fake smile on her face froze even wider. Without realizing it, she was mimicking the grin of the skull in the display case. "I wouldn't know," she croaked, taking a step back.

If Mulder was registering the maid's horrified reaction to his question, he didn't show it. "Can you open it?" he asked.

"I don't have a key," the woman said quickly.

Mulder nodded and looked back at the

cabinet. Suddenly he dropped his passive facade as he noticed something. On the carpet, below the cabinet doors, was a brownish-red stain. It could have been just about anything—a coffee stain, a spilled drink, a splotch of varnish . . .

Or it could be blood.

Mulder grabbed a small statue on a low table next to the cabinet. As he lifted the small idol, he could tell by its heft in his hands that it was made of cast iron.

Perfect.

BANG!

Mulder brought the statue down on the padlock sealing the cabinet.

"What do you think you're doing?" the maid screeched behind him. But she made no move to stop him.

BANG! BANG!

He hit the lock again and again, until the wood around it splintered. Mulder dropped the statue, and grabbed both doors of the cabinet. He flung them wide open.

Heads. Dozens of human heads were

inside the cabinet—facing him.

Mulder's first impression—one that he knew was wrong as soon as he had formed it—was that they were Halloween masks. They would have been the most frightening he had ever seen. The eyes and mouths of all the faces were sewn shut with thick black thread in crisscrossing stitches. Some of the heads looked quite old and in poor condition. Mulder could see the white gleam of skull shining through in spots where the skins had torn or deteriorated. Others looked much fresher. On all of the heads, male and female, the hair was still intact. It was a display worthy of any monster maker in Hollywood.

But they weren't masks. Mulder knew it even before he recognized George Kearns's face on the second shelf near the front.

These were Chaco's trophies. Heads from the victims of the cannibals of Dudley.

Mulder turned around. The maid was gone. He hadn't heard her go, but it didn't surprise him that she hadn't hung around.

He walked out of the small room, leaving the cabinet doors open wide, and climbed the stairs, wondering if Walt Chaco would be up to seeing him now.

Scully had just been upstairs herself, in Doris Kearns's house. No one was there.

As she headed down the stairs the phone in her pocket chirped. She holstered her gun and pulled out her phone.

"Scully," she said.

"It's me," Mulder said on his end. "Chaco's not here."

Scully reached the bottom of the stairs and turned her flashlight toward the living room, intending to take one more sweep through the ground floor to look for any clues.

"Yeah," she agreed. "Mrs. Kearns is missing too. But I don't think she left on her own. The power was off when I got here . . ."

Scully couldn't see, from where she stood, the man hiding in the living room, listening to her every word. It was Walter Chaco, and he had a tire iron gripped in his hands.

"And her car is still in the driveway," Scully added.

She could hear Mulder sigh on the other end. "Chaco must have taken her," she heard him say.

Then, as she passed through the living room doorway, she heard no more.

SLAM! Chaco brought the tire iron down on her head. Scully crumpled, dropping her phone and flashlight on the way down.

Chaco stood over her, sweating, breathing heavily. He saw her forehead bleeding where he'd hit her.

He didn't think he'd killed her. He hoped not. The beheading ritual was only effective if the victim was still alive. And conscious.

He bent down, grabbed her feet, and began dragging her to the door.

Over the cell phone, Mulder heard the sound of the blow that his partner had just taken.

"Scully!" he shouted. "Scully! Are you there? Answer me!" His voice got louder and more desperate with every unanswered plea. "Scully!"

He glanced out the window of Chaco's bedroom. In the distance, over the treetops, he could see a bright orange glow.

There was a bonfire burning out there. He guessed, from the direction he was facing, it was in one of the fields bordering I-40.

That could mean only one thing.

Chapter Thirteen

Scully regained consciousness in the passenger seat of a speeding car. She felt something covering her mouth, and after twisting her lips, she realized it was a wide piece of tape. She also discovered that her wrists had been tied together behind her.

Chaco was driving like a madman, pushing the car down a bumpy, winding country road.

Then Scully saw her gun on the seat between them.

Slowly she began to twist her arms around to the side, to try to reach it. If she could grab it, even with her hands behind her back, she might be able to—

But Chaco saw her moving and reached out and hit her. Scully's head flew back and knocked against the glass of the passenger-side window.

Chaco scooped up the gun with his right hand and held on to it as he steered the wheel.

"Don't try anything!" Chaco yelled at her. "Don't even think about it!"

But Scully wasn't listening. Through the windshield, she could see their destination up ahead: a huge bonfire burning in a field by the side of the road. She could see, in the light of the wicked, flickering flames, dozens of people circling the fire. She knew what that meant for her, if she couldn't figure a way out of this. She was, quite literally, dead meat.

Chaco parked the car some distance from the bonfire. He jumped out, ran around to Scully's side, and dragged her from the vehicle.

The air was cold, and the wind rushed by with a howl. The top of the tall fire twisted and spat sparks into the wind.

They were passing small clusters of people

now. Scully recognized some of the faces from the processing plant. They stood in small groups, talking informally, clearly enjoying themselves as they ate a meaty stew from paper plates.

A churning began in the pit of Scully's stomach as she realized what they must be eating. Or rather, *who*.

Doris Kearns . . .

The people barely acknowledged her or Chaco as the two of them passed by. Under other circumstances, she thought, she and Chaco would surely have been hard to ignore—Scully with a silver strip of duct tape over her mouth, stumbling across the field with her arms tied behind her; Chaco with his eyes darting this way and that, waving a gun in his free hand. But maybe this was a common sight for this group.

Scully heard someone talking as they passed, and the rest of the small group broke out in loud guffaws. She realized with a start that the man had just told a joke. It was as if they were at a Sunday picnic or town social—not engaging in a taboo as old as humankind.

Scully and Chaco kept walking, the fire looming up in front of them. Scully could see that a large number of the townspeople were still standing in line, holding paper plates, waiting to be served. They were moving, one at a time, up to a huge stockpot. Scully's eyes, already wide with fear, opened further when she saw that the chef was Dr. Randolph. He ladled out healthy portions from the pot to the hungry people.

When they reached the front of the crowd, Chaco stopped moving and pulled Scully to a halt with him. "What have you done here?" he cried.

Some of the people looked up at him curiously, but most kept eating and socializing among themselves, ignoring the raving old man.

"I warned you!" he shouted. "I said not to touch her!" He looked around wildly. A few more people were looking at him now, with hard expressions. Almost as if he was spoiling their fun.

"Doris Kearns was one of us!" he yelled at the solemn faces around him. "Who's behind this?"

The crowd parted, and Jess Harold walked toward them. The white bandage on his neck shone brightly in the flickering light. Harold stopped, then in an almost absurdly dainty gesture, he patted his lips gently with a paper napkin.

"Why didn't you listen to me?" Chaco asked, sounding disappointed. Sounding defeated. Then he shook Scully roughly, as he proclaimed, "It's the outsiders we have to deal with—not one of our own!"

Jess Harold lowered the napkin and smiled. His eyes were glazed and glassy. Suddenly his smile quivered, and one side of his face began to tic.

Scully suspected that he, too, was coming down with Creutzfeldt-Jakob.

"We'll deal with them all," Harold finally

said, trying to gain control of himself.

Chaco pushed Scully away. She tripped and fell to her knees.

But Chaco paid no attention to her. Suddenly, *he* became the focus of the crowd. He turned away from Harold, appealing directly to the townspeople. They had all gathered around him now, their faces unsmiling, their expressions defiant.

"Look at yourselves! Look at what you've become!" he intoned, trying to reach them. Trying to make them obey him once again, through the sheer power of his will. As they used to. "This isn't faith anymore—you're acting out of fear. You've turned this into an abomination."

But the people around him did not flinch or back down. Their faces remained unmoved. It was Chaco who gasped, realizing for the first time just how much of his power had slipped away.

Jess Harold took a step forward. "*You* brought in the one who made us all sick," he spat out, with venom in his voice.

But Scully could see Chaco wasn't ready to give up yet. Not without a fight. Not without another appeal to the people. His people.

"Once you turn on yourselves, it's over," Chaco cried. "How long before it's any one of us? Any one of *you?*"

He was starting to get through to them. They began to look at one another, then down at the ground, ashamed. Scully could see they were reconsidering their choice. He was reaching them.

But not all of them, and not soon enough. He hadn't reached Jess Harold. "That's not your problem anymore, old man," Harold said with a smug smirk.

Scully looked at Harold and saw a tall figure rise up behind him—someone wearing a primitive tribal mask and holding a wide, sharp blade in his hands.

Harold stepped aside and the masked figure moved forward.

Chaco raised the gun and aimed it at the

man in the mask. "No!" he screamed.

Chaco took a step back, and two of the locals grabbed him roughly, pointing the arm that held the gun up into the air. Harold moved in and took the gun away from him.

The two men stood facing each other, separated by inches. Sparks from the nearby fire wafted between them.

"If you kill me . . ." Chaco began, his voice quivering. He had to swallow before he could finish the sentence. "You kill us all."

Harold simply smiled and wordlessly jerked his head toward the fire. The two men holding Chaco nodded, and dragged him toward the burning timbers.

Scully wondered briefly if they were about to burn him alive. But then she saw them force Chaco to his knees near the fire and fasten his head into some kind of restraint. It was a narrow metal platform set on a short pole that had been pounded into the ground. A hinged metal band rose from the platform and this was clamped down over the back of Chaco's head. This gave the masked executioner a clear shot with his wide blade at the back of Chaco's bared neck. It was a clever device. Once the blade sliced cleanly through its target, the body would fall away while the head would remain firmly in place, held by the metal clamp. Undamaged. Ready to be displayed.

While everyone's attention was focused on the activity near the fire, Scully, still kneeling on the ground, began to squirm away from the fire on her knees. She wished that her hands were free, so she could crawl faster. If she could just put some distance between herself and the fire—blend into the darkness . . .

But no such luck.

Two of the townsfolk saw her. They quickly grabbed her and jerked her roughly to her feet. Scully looked wildly at the people holding her—the man on her left was Dr. Randolph. He and his companion half led, half dragged Scully back to the fire, to watch Chaco's execution.

Chaco was kneeling, bent over the platform, his head held firmly in place by the restraint. He wasn't even struggling—apparently he'd seen this happen enough times to know it would be useless.

The man in the tribal mask planted his legs, taking a firm stance, and heaved the ceremonial ax high above his head. Scully shut her eyes.

But she couldn't shut her ears.

She heard the high-pitched whistle as the blade sliced through the air, heard it even above the roar of the wind and the crackling of the fire. Then she heard the whistle end in a soft wet *crunch*, as skin, muscle, bone, and nerve were severed in an instant by the razor-sharp edge of the iron blade.

This was followed a moment later by a dull *thud*, which Scully knew was the sound of Chaco's headless body hitting the ground.

Her mind started spinning now. Her last chance to escape had already slipped away. She didn't dare open her eyes as she was pushed forward.

She heard the hinge of the curved metal

band groan as it was opened. *They must be taking Chaco's head out now*, she thought. She tried to pull away one last time, but too many people were holding on to her, too many hands were pushing her down. Too many hands were holding her in place as the metal strap was forced down around the back of her head.

The latch on the end of the strap made a decisive *click* as it locked into place. The crowd grew silent. All Scully could hear now was the sound of the wind and the crackling fire.

She felt, more than heard, the vibration of heavy footsteps. *That must be the big man in the tribal mask moving into position*, she thought.

Whoosh.

She heard the blade swing by her on its way up. The executioner was holding it over her head now, ready to bring it down. Ready to plunge it through her neck. The crowd became, if it was possible, even more still.

Strangely calm, almost feeling her consciousness begin to rise out of her body, Scully was ready for the end.

So the gunshots caught her by surprise.

BANG! BANG!

She snapped her eyes open while the sound of the second shot still reverberated in the air. She had opened her eyes in time to see the heavy ax tumble from the executioner's hands, landing on the ground a few feet away from her.

Then the big man in the primitive mask slowly crumpled over backward, mortally wounded.

Screams filled the air. The townspeople began to run madly from the scene. Scully craned her eyes as far to the left as they were able to go.

Mulder, his gun held in both hands in front of him, was advancing toward her. Slowly the realization sank in that she had been saved.

She saw legs dashing by—she didn't know how many people were there in the clearing, but it seemed as if all of them were running past her at once. Occasionally, through spaces between them, she could catch glimpses of Mulder getting closer.

Her eyes searched for and found the ancient blade lying harmlessly on the grass. No one was stopping to pick it up to finish the job. It was over.

But then, off to her right, she saw one other person standing still. She could see the square of bandage gleaming on his neck. It was Jess Harold.

And he had her gun. Slowly he raised his arm and aimed it in Mulder's direction.

Scully turned her eyes back to Mulder. He was still coming closer. But his eyes were focused on her—he didn't see the danger.

Scully tried to warn him. Shouting out the danger was impossible with her mouth taped shut, but she tried to warn him with her eyes and her body. The message didn't seem to be getting through. As he continued to come ever closer, he probably thought she was just struggling to be free.

But then fate smiled on Mulder.

As Harold held the gun out at arm's length, a fleeing woman ran by too close and knocked the gun from his hand.

Harold dove to the ground after the weapon. As he reached out for the gun, the heavy work boot of another fleeing townsperson crunched down on his outstretched hand, grinding the joints in his fingers and breaking the bones. Harold screamed in agony. Then an errant knee struck the side of his head, and he sprawled to the ground. More feet kicked and tripped and trampled over him as the townspeople made their escape.

Mulder rushed the last few feet toward his partner and quickly released her head from the metal clamp. Scully, still on her knees, straightened up. Her eyes roved wildly over the field, until they came to rest on the crushed body of Jess Harold. In the fury of its mindless stampede, the crowd had trampled him to death.

Mulder peeled the tape off her mouth. "Are you all right?" he asked her. Scully nodded, as Mulder untied her arms.

Then they both stood and looked around, surveying the site where the ancient ritual had invaded the modern world. They would catalogue the site. They would measure it. They would describe it and report it.

But they would never fully comprehend it.

The crowd had receded into the distance. All Mulder and Scully could see of them were pinpoints of light—the lanterns that some of the people held—bouncing madly across the field.

The two agents walked a few short steps to where the executioner in the tribal mask lay on the ground, with two bullet holes in his chest.

Mulder glanced at Scully, then crouched down and lifted the mask.

The man's eyes were open in death, and the corners of his mouth were still turned up in his habitual boyish grin. But the orange light from the flickering bonfire, reflecting on his teeth, cast an otherworldly aura on his face. It was Sheriff Arens.

"Where's Chaco?" Mulder asked as he stood up.

They looked around, eventually circling the fire. But Chaco's body was nowhere to be seen.

Chapter Fourteen

The next day began, interestingly enough, with business as usual at the Chaco Chicken processing plant. Workers lined up at their stations on the chicken line; trucks were loaded and dispatched.

But only a few minutes into the first shift, a motorcade of state troopers came screaming up the access road toward the plant, sirens blaring.

Troopers jumped out of their vehicles and rushed into the plant.

"Stand away from your work stations!" the trooper in charge shouted through a bullhorn.

The workers dutifully obeyed, and watched silently as two troopers rolled out a bright yellow ribbon, imprinted with the words POLICE LINE—DO NOT CROSS.

Mulder watched as Scully led the state police down the line of workers, pointing out the ones she recognized from the night before. Mulder stayed on the sidelines as the local police did their job, arresting the people his partner pointed out.

Scully watched with grim satisfaction as Dr. Randolph was led away in handcuffs. She could tell just by looking at him that the disease had progressed rather rapidly. Judging from the look in his eyes, he would be dead from Creutzfeldt-Jakob within the week.

As Scully went down the line of workers, she thought about the futility of what she was doing. There were so many people there last night, and so few faces she could positively identify. But it really didn't matter. As in the case of Dr. Randolph, nature itself would take care of those she missed.

The machinery of the plant went silent and the chicken line ground to a halt. The troopers had shut off the plant's power. Mulder wandered through the now almost quiet plant. Through a window, he saw some workers out back whom the troopers hadn't reached yet. They didn't know that work was over for the day.

The workers outside were moving with plastic buckets loaded with feed toward the rows of chicken cages. Well, Mulder supposed, that was a chore that would have to continue in any case, whether the plant was shut down or not. They couldn't just let the chickens starve to death.

"Fox Mulder?"

Mulder turned to see who had called his name. It was one of the state troopers, with an envelope in his hand. Mulder took it and opened the envelope.

It contained a fax of Walter Chaco's war records. *That was quick,* Mulder thought. He had wired in his request to the Department of Defense late the night before. He was grateful that they had expedited it, although it seemed pointless now.

He scanned over the information. The documents confirmed that Chaco had spent time with the Jale tribe in New Guinea.

Apparently, a transport plane he had been piloting during the Second World War had been shot down. Chaco was the only survivor.

He had spent six months with the tribe, which even the dry military record noted was surprising, as the tribe was suspected of cannibalistic practices. Mulder thought to himself that Chaco's charisma must have transcended language and culture barriers.

Mulder leafed through the other pages of the fax, and saw something that brought him up short. It impressed him enough that he strolled over to Scully, who wasn't nearly finished with the line of workers yet.

"Excuse me," he said to the trooper at Scully's side, and he put the papers in front of her. His finger pointed to the line that had caught his eye.

Walter Chaco's year of birth. 1901.

"You know, he looked pretty spry for a man in his nineties," Mulder whispered. "Didn't look a day over sixty."

Scully silently met his eyes, then moved on with the trooper, heading toward the next group of employees.

As Mulder watched her move on down the line, his thoughts flickered briefly back to Chaco. Scully had told him what had happened to the old man last night, yet his body wasn't found near the others. Mulder wondered where they would eventually find it.

The workers out back moved among the rows of chicken coops, unaware of what was happening inside the plant. Thousands of birds passed through here every day, and it was the workers' job to keep them happy until the next group came along.

One worker struggled with his heavy plastic bucket, and he had to put it down for a moment to catch his breath. He'd been feeling pretty lousy lately. He could feel himself sweating. His coveralls felt clammy and they clung to his skin. And now he was getting the shakes.

All he wanted to do was get his job done

and go home. He didn't care about the birds. Or what was going to happen to them after he'd fed them.

And he surely gave no thought to the feed he was about to offer them—a combination of seed, commercial meal, and the cooked remains from the feed grinder. He just wanted the birds to eat up so he could get out of there.

He picked up the bucket and carried it over to the chute that would deposit a carefully measured amount into each cage in his row. As he lifted the bucket to the funnel, something inside caught his eye. Something fluttering.

The man reached a gloved hand into the bucket and pulled out a tuft of gray-white hair. Human hair.

Funny, he thought. He opened his hand, but the hair stuck to his moist glove. He flicked his fingers lightly until the tuft fell free, and he watched it flutter away in the gentle breeze. *Someone oughta be more careful.*

Then he tipped the bucket into the funnel, and watched as the meal and seed and feed tumbled down the chutes toward the hungry, hungry birds.

The End

Read all of the X-Files Young Adult books:

The X-Files #5: **Empathy**
by Ellen Steiber

Lucy looked down to find that her uniform was spattered with blood. Dark, red, thick blood. Hesitantly she touched her hand to her face. And felt something warm. And wet. She drew her hand down—it was covered with blood as well.

It's just a nose bleed, Lucy told herself.

She was wrong. Her eyes fluttered shut, her knees buckled, and she fell to the floor, shaking. Strangers gathered around, staring down at her.

Lucy began to speak in slurred, trancelike words: ". . . nobody's gonna spoil us nobody's gonnaspoilusnobody'sgonnaspoilusnobody's gonnaspoilusnobody'sgonna . . ."